One Day

in the life of a software engineer...

P. Nirupam Pratap Reddy

Cedar books

Published by

Cedar books

An Imprint of

Pustak Mahal®

J-3/16, Daryaganj, New Delhi-110002

☎ 23276539, 23272783, 23272784 • ***Fax:*** 011-23260518

E-mail: info@pustakmahal.com • ***Website:*** www.pustakmahal.com

Sale Centre

▪ 10-B, Netaji Subhash Marg, Daryaganj, New Delhi-110002

☎ 23268292, 23268293, 23279900 • ***Fax:*** 011-23280567

E-mail: rapidexdelhi@indiatimes.com

▪ **Hind Pustak Bhawan**

6686, Khari Baoli, Delhi-110006

☎ 23944314, 23911979

Branches

Bengaluru: ☎ 080-22234025 • ***Telefax:*** 22240209

E-mail: pustak@airtelmail.in • pustak@sancharnet.in

Mumbai: ☎ 022-22010941, 022-22053387

E-mail: rapidex@bom5.vsnl.net.in

Patna: ☎ 0612-3294193 • ***Telefax:*** 0612-2302719

E-mail: rapidexptn@rediffmail.com

Hyderabad: ***Telefax:*** 040-24737290

E-mail: pustakmahalhyd@yahoo.co.in

ISBN 978-81-223-1134-1

Edition 2010

Printed at : Param Offsetters, Okhla, New Delhi-110020

Contents

Dedicated to
my fellow Techies

Preface

One fine evening, my wife and I were on our way back home when our car got stuck in a traffic jam. To keep ourselves entertained, we started narrating to one another some random love stories that we witnessed at our places of work. At some point, the discussion veered off from fact to fiction. We started mixing fact with fiction and started asking ourselves, 'What if' something like this was to happen? That was when the main storyline of this book cropped up between us. After we reached home, I felt that I can write a short story based on the idea. I wrote a couple of pages and showed the script to my wife. She liked it so much that she started insisting I write a novel based on the idea and not a short story. Initially I did not take it seriously, as I thought I was a busy guy with no time to spare for other activities. As it would always be, it is difficult not to do something when your wife has already decided about it. My wife took the script to my parents and they liked it too and all of them encouraged me to complete the work. Initially, I thought I will be done with the book in a couple of months but it took me six long months to finish it. Though it took me a long time, I would still say that I loved the activity. If not for the encouragement that I received from my parents and wife, I would have never dared to write something this big. I will always remain thankful for the support and encouragement that I received from them. I also thank my brother and my cousin for going through the first draft and giving me their valuable suggestions.

Finally, before I conclude, I have to mention that I enjoyed writing this book and so have the people who read it. I hope that you will enjoy it too.

—Pratap

Chapter 1

The Day Begins

6:00 a.m.

Tring! Tringg!! Tringgg!!! The alarm was furious. Ravi who had set the alarm to 6:00 a.m. was fast asleep and the alarm was doing its best to wake him up. After constantly trying to remind him about the eight o'clock meeting, the alarm decided to take some rest.

Meanwhile, Ravi was in a world where he was living the 'Axe' advertisement. As a matter of fact, he had been so influenced by the advertisement that he bought a bottle of 'Axe' just the day before.

His dream was full of action. He had just finished applying the deodorant when girls from all over the world started running towards his home. They were banging his door and trying to break into his house. The dream was filling Ravi with excitement. He was fast asleep but was grinning widely at the same time.

The girls had managed to break into his apartment and one of them was about to give him a kiss. The girl's lips were just a centimetre away from Ravi's lips, when suddenly the girl's face transformed into something long-familiar.

A noise had distracted him and it seemed to have triggered that change. Ravi was shocked with the change that happened and moved back. The girl had transformed into Praveen. Now instead of trying to kiss him, the character was asking him for status updates. The noise was getting louder and louder in the background.

Shocked with the change, Ravi woke up with a start. The change was so shocking that he started sweating. His entire dream was erased in a single shot but that strange sound continued. It was repeatedly going beep...beep...beep...when all of a sudden he realised that it was his mobile phone which was ringing.

He picked up the phone and rubbing his eyes with his hand said, "Hello!"

"Ravi! This is Praveen. Where are you now? Do you remember that there is a meeting at 8:00 a.m.? When are you planning to come to the office? I just wanted to make sure that you wake up on time for the meeting."

Ravi was a software developer at the Software Only Solutions (SOS, an acronym which sounded like a cry for help from clients who approached the company when in trouble), an Indian software consultancy firm, and Praveen was Ravi's boss. Yesterday Praveen had specifically mentioned to the entire team that there was an important meeting with the US-based client and it was important to be on time.

But when Ravi returned home in the night, he was excited to find that the 'BitTorrent' application on his computer had just finished downloading a new movie. It was already 11:00 in the night and he had to choose between sleep and the movie. As it would always be – his passion to watch a movie beat the idea of going to sleep.

By the time he realised that it was a good idea to sleep, it was already two o'clock. So, the morning's call from Praveen made Ravi start cursing his enthusiasm to watch movies, work in general and his alarm for not making a louder noise.

"Praveen, I will start by 7. I will be on time, don't worry," he said. "Thanks and bye."

Ravi was always irritated by the amount of over-enthusiasm Praveen showed towards managing his team. Today the irritation reached its crest because he was woken up when something really wonderful was going to happen in his dream.

'The good days in my life are over. As a student, I never got up at 6:00 for anything. Now my managers are not even giving me the time to finish my dreams! How great would it have been to be a student eternally! No office, no managers and no bugs. I think every good phase in life has to end sometime,' he thought.

But one great quality that humans share is the ability to forget. Ravi had forgotten too. Especially those days of his school and college life when he thought 'that phase of his life was difficult'. As a school going kid, he wanted to grow and become someone like his dad. 'The day I become as big as my dad, I will have freedom. Today everyone tells me to study. I have to get up on time for school and catch the school bus. I have to complete the homework and tuition work. The day I grow up I will never study...I will always play cricket.'

Having passed that phase came the senior secondary phase, when it was time to prepare for the JEE, AIEEE etc. 'God! What is this? I have to attend special classes, solve hundreds of problems, and attend mock tests...bullshit! I am feeling choked with all this work.'

After entering the engineering school, he thought life would be easy. So easy that he could bunk classes, watch movies, and run errands with friends. But a dismal first year performance changed all that. He understood that life wasn't so easy after all. He had to slog to complete his assignments, prepare for tests and interviews. During this phase, he always thought, 'One day I will become a software engineer, earn in dollars, buy a BMW or a Porsche and live a king's life. Life will be easy after engineering. I will never have to slog so much.' Thinking that software engineers live like kings, he prepared with grit and determination and got selected to SOS.

But little did he understand that in trying to achieve his childhood goal of 'never studying after becoming big...,' he entered a profession where he had to keep studying for the rest of his life. 'JAVA, C, C++, C#, Ruby, Perl, Python, PHP, Unix, Windows, VB, .NET, SQL Server, Oracle, J2EE, Beans, JavaScript, Jscript, periodical upgrades to these languages...' and the list goes on and on and on. The day you sign up for this career, you have signed up for a life of eternal learning.

After getting into his dream job, Ravi now saw the reality. His expectations from a software job were partially true. As a software engineer, he wasn't getting enough money to buy a BMW or a Porsche, but he did get enough to buy an Xbox 360 and the latest version of NFS. And it was better when compared to playing with a pirated version of NFS on a PC; yet it was nowhere near his original dream.

Ravi was employed with the company for the past three years. As is the case with most of the Indian software engineers, Ravi was living with two other friends at Gayatri apartments. The apartments were situated in Ameerpet which was around 15 kilometres away from his office situated in Gachibowli.

He got up and without opening his eyes groped his way to the mirror. He opened his eyes to see his own face in the mirror. His eyes were red and his face was a bit swollen, all indicating his insufficient sleep. Apart from that, Ravi looked as good as ever. He was a medium built person with a tummy which was growing round and round with every passing year. Though he wasn't fat, he was still conscious about his changing physique. He felt for the increasing fat around his stomach and thought, 'I should go to the gym. I think this is the reason why girls are not showing any interest in me. I think they like bodies with six pack abs.' But with work schedules like his, achieving a six pack abs was just akin to achieving a perfect score in any competitive exam such as JEE.

He was a typical software engineer, who apart from having a great problem solving brain had no other great attribute which would have put him apart from a group of similar software engineers.

He put on his specs and felt satisfied that this day had at least begun on a positive note. On a similar occasion, such as the one he was preparing himself for today, he first looked at Vijay's face and the day ended on a disastrous note. So, from that day onwards he stopped taking chances.

Taking his gaze away from the mirror, he looked at the clock and it showed 6:15 a.m. He still had time to get ready.

Ravi took his brush and looked around for the toothpaste. 'Where is it? Where did Vijay put it today?'

He searched around and found it near the dining table. 'I am sick of these people. I keep this place tidy and proper and these people spoil it. Maybe I should give another lecture to Vijay this weekend.'

Ravi continued with his morning activities and was finishing his bath when he heard Vijay shouting to him, "I am leaving for office. Bye. And by the way I am borrowing your bike today."

Ravi had just finished applying soap and was pouring water on his face. The last statement of Vijay shook him. Wiping his face he shouted, "Hey wait... I need my bike today. I have some urgent work..."

Ravi did not hear any response and he shouted again, "Vijay... Vijay, are you there?" Not getting any response, Ravi finished his bath and coming out of the bathroom looked around for Vijay.

'Damn it! He left. How can he take my bike without my permission? I am going to bash him tonight.' He looked at the clock and it showed 6:35 a.m. 'God! I am getting late. The only option that I have now is the 7 o'clock bus. I have to hurry now, otherwise the bus will not wait,' he thought. He went to his room and searched for the newly ironed shirt.

"Where is it? I have kept it right here!" After searching for a couple of moments, reality dawned upon him.

"Vijay took it! This is the fifth time in two weeks. I am going to kill him! #&@$$#O!^... I got that dress purposefully ironed for today and how can he do this to me? What should I do now!" Ravi was astonished.

Maybe, looking at his own face as the first thing in the morning wasn't such a great idea after all. Dejected, he searched for another shirt and after wearing it he looked at the clock and it showed 6:40. He hurriedly put on his trousers, socks and shoes and rushed out. While coming out, he made it a point to take some cash and his debit and credit cards along with him.

He locked the apartment and started walking towards the bus stop which was just five minutes away.

He was still cursing Vijay for pinching his shirt and bike. At the same time, he thought, 'I am sick of this company! Walking to the bus stand at 7 in the morning, dressed like a salesman! Yuck! What a uniform? How cool would it have been to go to the office dressed in something casual?'

As a matter of fact, he hated this formal attire today because on occasions like what he was preparing for today, he thought he would have carried a better impression in t-shirt and jeans.

The fact that Vijay had pinched his shirt made him feel worse and he tried hard to forget the painful fact. He instead tried to concentrate on more important issues. Today he was preparing himself for a very important occasion.

'I am going to take Naina on a date today. I have already asked her yesterday whether she could come with me for dinner today and she said she will come if she doesn't have work at office. I will have to somehow convince her for the dinner,' thought Ravi.

'Naina', the name filled Ravi with a sense of joy. It was only last week that she joined the project. He still remembered that lucky Wednesday when Praveen took her around the cubicles introducing her to everyone in the project.

"Hi Ravi...meet Naina. She is joining our project today and will be working on the User Interface. Since you have considerable experience with our UI, I thought it might be a good idea for you to help her."

"Hi Naina. I will definitely help her Praveen. Naina, please feel free to drop by whenever you have questions."

The smile that Naina gave him that day made him fall head over heels for her.

'How lucky! I am going to be her mentor. Yahoo!' thought Ravi.

From that day onwards, Ravi always made it a point to spend at least an hour everyday with her. Having failed twice before in matters like these, this time he decided to be quick with his proposal. His past experiences gave him such valuable lessons that he was putting all that learning into practice over the past one week.

Today he was ready. He was ready with the cash and the cards. He was ready with the courage to ask her for a dinner. And above all ready with the 'Axe' spray which he bought yesterday for this very occasion. He was sure that today he will be lucky and will definitely make a positive impression on her.

As he walked around the corner, he saw the street dog sleeping on the pavement. Till a few months ago, Ravi was a dog lover but one incident changed all that. Today the sight of the dog again triggered one painful memory.

Five months ago, after a day of heavy work, he got down from his office bus at 8:30 in the night and was walking towards his apartment. He was dejected and Praveen's voice was ringing in his head.

'Ravi, you don't know how to solve this silly issue? When I was a developer, I never used the word 'No' for anything. When I did not know the solution for any issue, I used to take it as a challenge and work that night and come with results. You on the other hand, do not show an iota of interest in any challenge. This is going to hurt your career, Ravi. Show more enthusiasm. Go now.'

At office, Ravi did not know how to confront Praveen but now he came up with an ingenious idea. He imagined Praveen's face in front of him and kicked a stone towards that imaginary figure.

Luck was something that was not on Ravi's side that day. The stone found its target.

'Bowww!!!'

That sharp sound made Ravi instantly realise his mistake. The stone hit a dog which was coolly taking a nap on the pavement. He initially tried to fool the dog by trying to walk as if he was not the one responsible for this, but the dog was not one to be fooled so easily and started chasing him.

Ravi did not remember how he dodged the dog that day but somehow managed to escape unhurt. But it so happened that one of his shoes had come off in that confusion and the dog carried it away in revenge. The painful experience of being chased by a dog, with everyone watching him was something which got etched permanently in his mind.

'Stupid Dog...looks like it will never leave this colony,' he thought and continued his walk. As usual Ravi was at the bus stand by 6:45 a.m. Give or take five minutes, he is always there at that time. There were many others like him dressed in their formals waiting for their respective company buses.

In addition to this software group, today a new beggar group had formed at the bus stop. Some kids from that group were begging for money, while the adults were taking rest on the pavement. "Sir...one rupee please," a five year old kid was begging and encouraged by Ravi's innocent face, the kid started going around him for money.

Ravi was not one to part with money so easily and hence waved off the kid. "Go, go...I don't have change...go..." and Ravi started moving around uneasily. But the kid was relentlessly bugging Ravi and after a minute decided that the strategy of begging was not working. He changed tactics and went into an attack mode. "Sir... please sir..." and he clutched onto Ravi's leg just as how a baby monkey would latch onto its mother's stomach.

Ravi was shocked. He noticed that the whole community at the bus stop was looking at him and giggling. A couple of people were going nuts with laughter.

"Hey...leave me now. Come on...hey...you...get off..." and Ravi was trying to pull that kid off his leg but the kid would not give up.

"Sir...one rupee sir...one rupee..." and clutched onto his leg harder.

Seeing that there was no other way of letting the kid go, Ravi pulled his purse out and gave him a rupee. The kid let his leg go and went off running.

‘Idiot! Spoiled my well-ironed trousers,’ and Ravi started dusting his trousers where the kid had latched onto it. Suddenly he heard a set of voices which sent a chill up his spine.

‘Sir...one rupee sir...’ Ravi looked up and saw that now there were four more kids standing in front of him asking him for a rupee each.

“Where did you come from?” Ravi asked exasperatedly. One of the persons standing beside Ravi said, “The kid whom you gave a rupee to, showed his prize to these kids and told them you gave it to him. Give them the money. If they get onto you just as the first fellow did, you will become a laughing stock here,” and he started laughing.

‘Idiots,’ thought Ravi and gave each of them a rupee. Initially when he arrived at the bus stand Ravi was in no hurry to board the bus, but the experience that he just now went through made him anxious for its arrival.

‘When will this bus come? Hope these four kids don’t come here with forty more people,’ he thought and started praying to God. ‘God...please send the bus as soon as possible.’

God answered Ravi’s prayer.

❖❖❖

Chapter 2

The Journey

7:00 a.m.

Screech...

The office bus reached the stop exactly on time. Ravi was overjoyed to see the office bus. He thought that he never felt such happiness before. Two people got in and Ravi was standing just two feet away from the bus door. He was taking those two steps to get in, when the bus started.

"Hey! Stop...stop the bus..."

Screech...

The bus stopped again after making Ravi run for around five feet.

"You...why didn't you wait for me?" Ravi demanded.

"I did not find you near the door," said the bus driver.

"What?! I was standing just a couple of feet away."

"I know, but I drive this bus according to my own rules. Everyday I stop the bus with the door facing that particular telephone pole. If I don't find you standing there I will not stop for you."

"What? I regularly board the bus at this stop and you say you don't know me? I will complain about this to your travel coordinator."

"Ha! Go and complain. As if I care."

Amazed with the driver's callousness, Ravi walked in and complained to the first passenger he met there.

"You heard the way he was talking?"

"The other day he did not stop for me. Compared to what happened to me, you were treated well."

Ravi was a bit surprised because he did not understand what his co-passenger meant by that statement.

'Is he feeling bad that the driver treated me differently from him or is he agreeing with the statement that the driver is rude? Anyway things like this are common in this bus and I better not continue my talk with this gentleman. Who knows what he will say next.'

Thinking this way, Ravi pulled out the earphones of his cellphone and plugged them into his ears. He tuned into a FM station. "Hi listeners, it is now 7:05 a.m. I am RJ Shiva and you are listening to Radio FM. Today's special programme is a chat show with our star hero Arvind, whose movie 'Hit' which we think is going to be a megahit is getting released today."

Ravi thought, 'Wow! Name of the movie itself is 'Hit' and the RJ is declaring the movie a hit even before the movie is released.'

"Sir, your last movie was a super-duper hit. How do you manage to be successful every time?"

"As you know, I come from a family of heroes so acting is kind of in my blood. Actually I don't act in my movies, it comes naturally to me and that is the reason for my success."

Ravi was surprised. He thought, 'What! Your last movie and a success? What was there in it to become a hit?! Bullshit!! I think I should have become an actor. Even when I code properly Praveen and my customer always find faults with me. No one recognises my hard work but public seems to be lapping up everything on the silver screen. Sigh! Life is not fair.'

The RJ continued, "Sir, so please tell us about this new movie 'Hit'. What is it like? What do you think makes it a 'Hit'."

"You know my latest movie is a class, mass, comedy, action, family and commercial entertainer. The movie starts with a chase sequence canned in America."

"America?"

"Yes. Why I am in America and who is chasing me is a suspense which is revealed only in the climax. You should see the stunts which I did. They were fantastic."

The RJ praised the hero more by saying, "Yes sir, we know they will be fantastic. The action sequences in your previous movie were really awesome. But sir one question, why did you choose America for your chase sequence? Does the story involve any elements from outside India?" the RJ enquired.

The hero was pleased with the praises from the RJ but still he could not entertain questions which dealt with the storyline. So he said, "Thanks for the compliments but I cannot reveal the entire story on radio here. If you want to know more about my movie, then please watch my movie in the theatre." And again he went into a self-appreciating mode. "This time there are scenes where I fight with hundred people at the same time. They came out so well that you will be stunned when you watch them on the big screen."

"Sir, our listeners and especially your fans will be interested in knowing what is the storyline of the movie. Any hint would be great, sir," prodded the RJ.

The hero was more generous this time. For my fans, he thought and gave a hint as to what the movie was about. "This time the movie is a suspense thriller. In the first half of the movie, I portray the character of a software engineer and the second half reveals who I really am."

"Software engineer?! But you said that the movie opens with a chase sequence?" asked the RJ in a surprised tone.

"That is the suspense element," laughed the hero. "Who is chasing me and why they are chasing me is something that you will know only when you watch the movie."

"Oh, ok..."

The hero started giving some more details and said, "Actually in the movie I am an amnesia patient. In the first half I am a person who has forgotten his past and is working as a software engineer. Throughout the first half I start searching for the person who spoiled my life, while how I take my revenge on that person forms the second part of the story."

"Wow!! Sounds an interesting storyline, sir," exclaimed the RJ, "so the movie is a revenge-based thriller where you take revenge on the person who made you forget your past. I got it."

"No, I take revenge on him because he made me become a software engineer," quipped the hero and said, "that was a joke!" and started laughing.

'Bullshit! What a stupid joke? Everyone makes fun of us. Yeah, if my company bus driver himself doesn't care about me, why should this hero care about us? But what a concept, he is a software engineer in the first half and he will show how the real hero should look like in the second half. So we can't be heroes, is it? I hope at least this movie is worth watching,' Ravi thought.

Just at the same moment, the bus passed by the side of a huge poster. Ravi looked out of the window and saw that it was the poster of the movie being discussed on the Radio. 'HIT' was written in bold letters on the canvas. The most striking feature on the entire canvas was the hero sitting bare-chested in front of a computer. On the poster, the hero was showing off his six-pack abs typing something on the PC.

Ravi looked at the hero's six-pack and involuntarily felt the flab around his ever growing tummy. The poster obviously did not impress him. It showed a vision which was too hard for him to digest.

'My life sucks,' he thought and went into an agitated mood. The poster had badly turned him off. 'I work hard daily and don't even get the time to eat or sleep properly. Here Bollywood shows six-pack software engineers! I will not watch this movie in the theatres. I will wait for the torrent,' he thought. But as was the case with him always, he quickly added a small rider, 'However, if the review is good. I will consider watching it in the theatre.'

But as a matter of fact, it has been a long time since he watched a movie on the very first day. He was a movie buff but at one point of time he started thinking that the reviews were more fun to read compared to the movies themselves. Also the pain to see a dumb-witted hero dancing with beautiful heroines when all that Ravi did for the whole day was coding, depressed him. He started questioning his own intentions for watching a movie. 'Why should I go to the theatre? What is the main reason? Is it for entertainment or for paying the producer and hero, so that the hero can dance with more girls?'

The obvious answer to that question was 'entertainment'. 'If it is for entertainment then am I getting entertained by watching every movie that is released?'

'Obviously not. Today's movie was such a crap that instead of the movie the comments passed on it by the people sitting behind me were more interesting. What a waste of money? From the next time onwards, I will come to a theatre only after reading the review.'

So today's advertisement with the hero was obviously not going to make him go to the theatre, but the poster was really a big turn off for him. 'By tomorrow the review will be out. The review will tell me whether I should go to the theatre or wait for the torrent,' thought Ravi.

The radio suddenly started blaring something into his ears.

"What! Is the signal weak here? What is this sound?"

"Listeners! This is the first song from the movie 'Hit'. Listen and enjoy," the RJ's voice interrupted the noise.

'Is it a song?! Where are the lyrics and where is the music? I am getting bored of this thing...' thinking this way Ravi switched channels and the next channel was playing some devotional songs.

Not in a mood to listen to those songs, he switched off the radio and peered out of the window. The morning sun was above the horizon and slowly warming up the cool morning air.

'What a pleasant morning. The traffic is also considerably less now, in another hour the roads will be overflowing with all sorts of vehicles. Though this bus comes too early to my place, it is a better option compared to the other modes of transport. But how great would it have been if I could drive my Pulsar in such a pleasant weather today.'

Thinking so, his heart started burning again. 'Oh damn! I had to come by the bus because of Vijay. Only if he hadn't taken my bike! Tonight I am going to surely kick his ass. Anyway, I will borrow Ananth's bike today.'

Ravi tried to console himself by thinking about the good reasons for not coming on his bike today. To console himself, he started recollecting the bad experiences that he had with his bike. This he thought would at least give him some consolation. He started from that point in history where he faced lots of hardship to buy a bike.

Three years ago, after graduating from college, Ravi started saving money for a bike. His dad had always denied Ravi one, when he was in college. So now with a job in hand and a good salary, Ravi was determined to buy a bike. After saving enough in five months, he bought a Bajaj Pulsar. Never having driven a bike before, he had some unforgettable experiences with it.

After a week's practice, Ravi planned a long drive on his bike. After crossing the Ameerpet junction, he started zooming towards Begumpet where he had his first accident. A buffalo came in front of him from nowhere. Not knowing how to balance his bike in a situation like that, he lost control of the bike and it rammed into the road divider. The buffalo walked away coolly but Ravi ended up with bruises. Also the pain of getting a new bike repaired in the very first month of its purchase made the experience worse.

The second experience was even weird. Ten months after the first accident, Ravi had become a good biker. He rode on his bike almost daily to office and used to do 'eights' and 'circles' in front of his friends to show them his biking prowess. Though the experience of driving on the pothole-ridden Hyderabadi roads was painful, he used to love his bike for the amount of freedom it gave him when it came to commuting within the city. But there was one experience which made him give up his bike for his daily commute to office.

One day Ravi was riding to office and was overtaking a bus from its left side, when suddenly something happened and he blacked out. When he woke up, he saw that he was in a hospital with a fractured hand and a fractured leg. He noticed that his parents had come all the way from his hometown to attend to him and a couple of his friends were also present in the room.

He pulled up some strength to speak and said, "Dad, what happened to me? The last I remember was overtaking the bus and now I am here...what happened?"

His dad walked to his side, sat beside him and said, "When you were trying to overtake the bus, at the same time someone was trying to get down from the running bus. As I heard from some bystander, the person who got down from the speeding bus landed in your lap and both of you suffered a good number of injuries. That person is also getting treated in another ward in the same hospital."

His mother was sobbing and said, "We told you not to buy that stupid bike and you did not listen to us. See what has happened to you. For our sake, promise me that you will not use the bike again...please..."

Seeing his mom's face that day Ravi decided not to use his bike unless it was urgently required. That was the reason why Vijay started using his bike and it had almost become Vijay's property for the last two years. So even today Vijay did not wait for Ravi's response before taking away his bike.

Having thought about those two painful experiences, Ravi felt a little better.

Screech...

The bus halted at another stop, somewhere near Banjara hills and Ravi looked at his watch and it showed 7:20.

'I will be in office in another 20 minutes. I think I will be the first person to enter the conference room. What should I do if I sit in the conference room before the others arrive?'

He was thinking this way when he heard someone shouting from the driver's side of the bus. The noises seemed to have attracted the attention of everyone in the bus, as Ravi noticed that everyone was looking in that direction. Apparently a woman employee who was getting into the bus requested the driver to wait for another friend of her (employee of the same company) who was on her way. The woman was telling the driver that her friend would be here in a minute and the driver did not listen to her. This led to a war of words between both the parties which attracted the attention of everyone in the bus.

"I will complain to your coordinator."

"Go and complain, according to my rules I shouldn't waste time at bus stops waiting for people who are still on their way. I am not making any mistake here."

"Hey, you have joined only last week and aren't being helpful to passengers. The previous driver was such a friendly guy. You are a rude fellow."

"What! You compared me to some other driver? You have insulted me. Get your 'previous driver friend' and get him to drive you to office."

"Hey! Why are you overreacting? What have I asked for? Just asked you to wait for another passenger and you are shouting at me like this? Are you sane? Are you drunk?"

"Listen lady, I am not here to take insults from people like you. If you wish to come, get in, otherwise stay out and come with your friend," shouted the driver.

"I will complain," was what the woman could shout which the driver found to be an amusing statement. Though two more male passengers got into an argument with him, he never listened. Meanwhile, as the argument continued the other woman passenger about whom the quarrel was going on managed to board the bus. Both the parties argued with each other for two more minutes and then everyone went quiet and got back to their seats.

The bus journey started again, but in just a few minutes the bus jerked to a sudden halt and everyone in the bus heard a loud crash which indicated the breaking of some windowpane.

Many people put their heads out of the bus windows and noticed that the bus driver who was in a very agitated mood had managed to hit a Wagon-R. The car's back was crushed by the impact and the window pane at the back of the car was smashed completely. The driver of the car had got down and was inspecting the damage. Obviously, he was not happy with what had happened to his car.

"You! You get down," he shouted at the bus driver.

The bus driver who was already in an agitated mood shouted back, "Get your car off the road. What are you staring at?"

The Wagon-R driver went crazy at the fact that the bus driver instead of apologising was arguing with him. He shouted back to him saying, "Get down, you idiot. Get down. I am not going to leave you today."

The time was 7:25 and Ravi was getting agitated with the way things were going on. It was just a few minutes ago that he thought he would be reaching office on time. But now if this fight continued for some more time he would definitely be late.

Meanwhile, the Wagon-R driver had become too agitated with the callous attitude of the bus driver and barged into the bus. Ravi heard him shouting, "Who is going to pay for the damage? Your dad?"

"You applied sudden brake in the middle of the road. It is your fault," shouted the bus driver.

"No, it is yours," shouted the car driver and he took the fight to a new level. He caught hold of the bus driver by his collar and slapped him. The bus driver too reciprocated and a fight ensued. Those two were fighting like WWE wrestlers when someone in the bus shouted, "Leave it man! You can claim insurance. Leave us now. We are getting late."

This incensed the car driver more and even while fighting, he shouted back, "Who is that? You pay me the damages and I will leave."

The fight had created a minor traffic jam and two passersby got into the bus and caught hold of both the drivers and brought the situation under control. They tried to mediate and after listening to both the parties they decided that it was the bus driver's fault and he had to be taken to the police station to register a complaint. Seeing that there were three people against him, the bus driver kept quiet. But the people in the bus started protesting that they would get late.

The car driver shouted back saying that he was not going to leave and that he was taking the bus keys with him. He pulled the keys, dropped them into his pocket and got down from the bus pulling the bus driver by his collar.

"Hey! Wait, wait...listen...where are you going? Wait..." People were shouting and this man wouldn't look back. He pushed the bus driver into his Wagon-R and requested the mediators also to come with him to which one of them readily obliged.

Not concerned with the fact that people from the bus were shouting at him, he turned a corner and was gone.

"What is this? How could something like this happen?" everyone seemed to be asking the same question.

Someone from the group got up and phoned the bus coordinator. He explained the situation to the coordinator and said, "What should we do now?"

"Sir, give me five minutes. I will talk to the bus company and will get back to you with a solution."

"Okay." And he ended the call.

"Hey everyone...listen...listen please...I have just now called the bus coordinator and he said he will tell us what to do in another five minutes."

Ravi overcomes with anxiety. It was already 7:35 and he had to attend the meeting at 8:00.

The bus coordinator called back and said, "Sir, apparently there are no other buses or drivers available at this moment."

"What should we do now?" questioned the passenger.

"Sir, a driver would be available only in another half an hour and by the time he arrives, it will be around 8:30. If you wish to wait till 8:30, we can provide a driver for you; else you can reach the office by your own means. That is the only thing we can suggest...again...we are very sorry for what happened, sir."

"8:30! That is too much! Also the bus keys were taken away by the person whose car was involved in the accident. What will that driver do if he comes here? Isn't there any other bus plying nearby?" he asked.

"No sir, I am afraid no buses ply here."

"At least tell us when you can send another bus here," he shouted.

"Wait for one minute, sir. I will check," and after a few seconds he got back and said, "only by 8:30 sir."

Having no other option the passenger replied, "Okay...I will convey this to the other passengers."

"Thank you, sir."

Meanwhile, the whole bus went silent and everyone was intently looking towards the person and showing eagerness to listen to what he had to say. So this time the person did not ask the people to listen to them, as they were already showing keenness.

"The bus coordinator is saying that he can send a new bus here only by 8:30. So, if you wish to stay here you can wait, else we can all leave by the APSRTC bus or autos."

One voice came up, "How can he say that? Wait...let me talk to him..." and another voice followed..."yes...we should talk to him again," and another, "yes...we should..."

Ravi felt that it was not a solution for him and he got down from the bus. As he was getting down from the bus, he heard someone from the group calling the vehicle coordinator. The caller started yelling at the coordinator.

"They cannot achieve anything except for yelling at the coordinator. Better I find an auto or a bus; else I cannot reach by eight. I think the bus stop is around the corner."

Meanwhile, the road was getting jammed. A couple of people got into the bus and enquired about the situation. After understanding the situation, one of them said, "At least let's push this bus aside. This way it is creating a major traffic jam here."

Some enthusiastic people from the bus agreed and after asking everyone to get down from the bus, they pushed the bus aside.

Meanwhile, Ravi managed to reach a bus stop. Fortunately for him, the bus stop was where he thought it would be and he waited for a bus to arrive. It was already 7:40 and he was definitely running late. The first bus that arrived was so full that about ten to fifteen people were already hanging from the footboard. Owing to the weight of the people, the bus tilted towards the footboard side and was moving at a snail's pace. Looking at the bus, Ravi did not feel like getting into it as he thought he would be crushed once he gets into it.

He left the bus and two more came in another 2 minutes but

they too were full like the previous one. Then an auto-rickshaw stopped beside him.

"Gachibowli," asked Ravi.

"Shared or normal?"

"Normal."

"150 rupees."

"What! I will pay by the meter. By the meter it will be only 75, I think."

"What meter? Sir, as a shared auto I will earn around 150 by the time I reach Gachibowli...now if I have to take only you to Gachibowli I will be at a loss. So, I will take you to Gachibowli only if you pay me 150 rupees. Also by operating my vehicle as a shared auto, my meter got broken. So there is no way of paying me 'by the meter'," saying this, the *auto-wallah* giggled.

"But...ok...then I will come by this shared mode. How much is it?"

"35 rupees...but you will have to wait. I will start only if there are 4 more passengers."

"Wait for more people! Okay, in that case I will get more people for you."

Saying this Ravi rushed to the place where his bus was stationed and he saw that there were still some people in the bus.

He got into the bus and said, "There is a shared auto waiting over there, is there anyone willing to take the option?"

"No, actually we are waiting for another bus. The coordinator promised to re-route another bus here. He said it will be here by 8:10 or 8:15, so we are waiting for it," said someone.

But Ravi was desperate to get more people to ride with him and said, "I bargained with him well. He agreed for rupees 35 per person to Gachibowli. With this option you will reach faster. Anyone who has some urgent meeting or work can come with me."

But none of them showed any interest. One of them even advised him, "This shared auto thing, it is a bit dangerous you know...I would advise you to stay back..." That person was still about to say something but Ravi got down from the bus. He was in no mood to wait and listen to some silly advices.

He rushed back to the auto and noticed that he had got a bit lucky. There were already four people sitting in the auto, but the only seat available to him now was the one beside the driver. It was already 7:50 and having no other option, he took it.

The ride was a tough one as the driver's seat was obviously designed only for him and not for the passengers. The original seat was extended by adding two more iron *dabbas* to the driver's seat. Apart from travelling, it is the duty of the passenger to keep that seat stuck to the auto. The *dabba* was wobbling whenever the driver made a sharp turn. Ravi was finding it difficult to find something to which he could hold on to.

'I hope this driver doesn't drive fast. I am unable to sit on this seat properly, if this fellow makes some stupid manoeuvres I will be rolling on the road that very next moment,' he thought.

It did not take much time for Ravi's fears to turn into reality. The driver, strictly adhering to the high standards of the auto driving community, was driving at top speed and was making some manoeuvres which would have put Schumacher to shame. Ravi closed his eyes and latched onto the rod beside the driver. He started praying to God and cursed his own stinginess.

'I should have paid him 150, I would have at least had a

comfortable ride then. Now if I fall down it will cost me more than that amount for the medicines and the hospital bills. Why don't I behave sensibly?'

After five minutes of the rough drive, Ravi noticed a muddy pool of water on the road. He realised that the driver was driving the auto directly into that pool at full speed.

"Hey...hey...slow down!" Ravi shouted. But before those words could be heard by the driver, the auto had managed to cut into the water and 'Splash!'

The water was splashed so high that some amount of it had been thrown into the auto too. In just a matter of two seconds, Ravi's well-ironed trousers were covered with mud.

"You idiot! I told you to slow down, right?"

"Sorry sir! Did not notice that pool of mud."

"What? You did not notice it? Look at what you have done to me."

The others in the auto empathised with Ravi's situation and scolded the auto driver. "See the road and drive. Poor fellow...see how he got drenched in that water," someone commented.

Ravi calmed down getting some sympathy from his co-passengers. Fortunately for him in the next five minutes someone from the rear seat got down and he shifted to that place. He felt more secure now.

The auto stopped somewhere near Madhapur. The auto was full but still the *auto-wallah* was greedy to load it with more people. A man and his fifteen-year old kid were standing there. After bargaining with the driver, the man adjusted himself in the already loaded front seat and the kid settled in Ravi's lap. Initially Ravi protested but the kid's dad said, "Just five minutes. We will get down near hi-tech city."

‘What a way to start the day?’ thought Ravi. He felt suffocated but there was no other option for him now. He had to bear all that for another fifteen minutes.

By the time he reached his office, it was already 8:15. He paid the auto and as he was rushing through the entry Gate 4 dusting the dried patch of mud on his trousers, the security guard stopped him.

❖❖❖

Chapter 3

The First Fight

8:20 a.m.

"Sir, show me your ID card please," the guard standing at the Gate 4 asked Ravi.

"Oh yeah...sure," Ravi put his hand into his shirt pocket and pulled out his ID card and showed it to the guard.

"One minute, sir...I need to check your bag too," and saying this, the guard took Ravi's bag and checked it.

"Sir, I found this pen drive in your bag and as per our security rules, it is not allowed into the campus. You should go to Gate 1, where they will deposit it in a temporary safe and you can collect it while going back."

"Yeah, I know that but I have to attend a meeting now. I am already late by 15 minutes. Walking to Gate 1 will take me another 5 to 10 minutes. Can you allow me for today? I will deposit the pen drive at Gate 1 later."

"No sir, I cannot do that. You have to go to Gate 1."

"Please..."

"No."

"Please, at least keep this pen drive with you. I will collect it from you later."

"I told you 'NO'. Please do not irritate me like this in the morning; it is not possible for me to keep this pen drive with me. If I lose it, it is an unnecessary tension for me, also our duties keep changing and I might not be here by the end of the day. It will be difficult for both of us to meet again. Now please go to Gate 1."

Seeing the authoritativeness with which the guard refused to allow him from Gate 4, Ravi thought, 'I envy you. At least you have a bit of authority at this gate. Look at me; no one listens to me in this company. Not my manager, not the security guard and not even my computer which keeps crashing day in and day out. God! What a job!' and started walking towards Gate 1.

Walking towards Gate 1, Ravi started thinking about the presentation which the SOS guys had given to him at his college. Three years ago, a team of recruiters from SOS had come to recruit students from Ravi's batch.

The PPT had just ended and it promised the students the earth, the moon and the heavens. "Listen students, we offer a pay package which is unrivalled in the industry. Not just the pay package but the opportunities you get in terms of work are mind-boggling. We work for clients which are big names in their respective areas, i.e., aviation, financial and banking sector, consulting. We have hundreds of the Fortune 500 companies as our clients, what else do you need?"

The students were mesmerised with the talk and all of them nodded in unison.

"As mentioned in our PPT, you will work on cutting edge technologies which will have a profound effect on the society. You will be responsible for key decisions which make or break our clients." The students imagined themselves in a world where they were treated akin to kings.

After joining SOS, Ravi realised that reality was much different from what that PPT had promised him. Being at the lowest rung of the ladder, there wasn't much decision making involved. You execute what is assigned to you. You never decide what is assigned to you. Also, being part of two scrapped projects in three years at SOS did not help him get a better impression about the industry in general.

'Not even the guard at the gate cares about me and that PPT told us that the engineering team would be the most valuable one in this company.'

'Cutting edge technologies,' I thought, 'I would develop something cutting edge; never thought that statement meant I should learn how to use a new tool every year.'

With these thoughts racing through his mind, Ravi arrived at the Gate 1. Just as he was depositing the pen drive, he saw an office bus arriving. Some people got down from it and Ravi noticed that they were the same people who travelled with him in the office bus half an hour back.

"Hi!" greeted the same person who had advised him to stay back and take the re-routed bus. "I thought you would have already reached. So, have you just arrived?" he asked in a jocular manner.

Ravi was aghast seeing how his idea of taking the auto had not given him any advantage.

In a surprised tone, he asked, "Oh! But you said that the re-routed bus would come only at 8:15."

"Actually just two minutes after you had asked us to take the shared auto, the coordinator called us again and said that they found another office bus which was plying nearby and re-routed it to our point. The bus arrived at 7:55. Also I wanted to tell you there itself, 35 rupees from that place to Gachibowli is too much. They charge you only 20 rupees," said that person. As he was saying this, he noticed that Ravi's trousers were covered in mud. "Oh! What happened? You are covered in mud," asked that person.

Ravi was shocked with the way things were going for him today. He gave a weak smile and said, "That is a long story. I have an urgent meeting to attend." He raced towards his building thinking, 'I have been cheated today.'

SOS had a sprawling campus of 40 acres at Gachibowli. They had built six different buildings on campus which housed around 3000 employees. The company had four gates for entry and exit. It was plush with lawns, had basketball, tennis and volleyball courts and also a swimming pool. Three of the buildings were six floors high and two of them were 8 floors high. The sixth building which was seven floors high served as a multilevel vehicle parking facility. This campus was the face of a new India which was much different from the vision of a land of slums, buffaloes and snake charmers cherished by Hollywood even today.

Ravi's team was located on the fourth floor of building no. 2. After reaching building no. 2, he noticed that there were a noticeable number of people waiting for the lifts. Hence, he thought it was a better idea to take to the stairs and raced up them. He was panting by the time he reached the Conference room 4138, where the meeting was taking place.

'8:30 a.m.' showed Ravi's watch. He was too late. He knew what was going to follow but he cannot avoid it. He knocked on the door and looked through the glass pane which flanked the door. He noticed Praveen waving to him to come in. Suddenly at this moment his mobile phone rang and Ravi cut off that call without even looking at who dialled him.

Ravi quietly opened the door and as he entered, he looked around to see who else was late, 'Except for Naina everyone is here; only I am late. Surely Praveen is going to shout at me after this meeting. Oh, what a way to start the day...'

Holding his conviction true, Praveen did not seem to be in a good mood today. The meeting was a teleconference with a US-based client. Generally the regular discussion happens with an Indian employee who represents SOS onsite, but it was a meeting directly with the client as a release of the updated version of the project was due on the coming Monday. The release indicated the end of the development cycle and the beginning of a test cycle. The client was reviewing the status of all the items that were due and whether the team was ready to meet the Monday deadline.

"So, Praveen you are saying that we are on track on all the aspects of the database and services. That is great news. What about the UI, we haven't talked anything about it till now. What are the updates on that portion?"

"Actually Carl, we have revamped the billing and procurement screens as per requirements. We are on track with the review screens. We are planning to finish that work by Friday. What do you think, Ravi?"

Ravi was about to say something when Carl interrupted him. "Praveen, this time we are following the test driven development model, right? What is the status with UI test automation?" Carl was about to complete his statement when the room was filled with the noise of a cellphone ringing.

Praveen tried to keep the focus on the meeting and said, "Oh that! Ravi, what is the status?" It was Ravi's mobile phone that was making the noise and Ravi was sitting with a shocked expression on his face. Praveen sternly looked at Ravi and that look conveyed enough information to Ravi. Ravi hurriedly reached for his mobile phone and switched it off.

"Uh! What is it?" Having been interrupted by the phone call, Ravi did not listen completely to what Praveen and Carl were discussing.

"That is why you should put your phone in silent mode when you come to a meeting. We are discussing about the UI, Ravi. Carl wants the status. What is the current status of the UI?" Praveen demanded.

"Yeah...review screen development wise we are on track. UI test automation is about 25% done."

Praveen pounced on that statement. He frowned, twisted his mouth and put a face which made Ravi tremble with fear. "What? Tests are only 25% complete? Ravi, do you know we have the release on Monday?"

"Yes...but...I...couldn't get enough time to both code and automate tests at the same time."

"So what? Okay...anyway Carl, we will take that offline between us. I will get this done by Monday."

"Are you sure, Praveen?" said Carl.

"Yes, I will get this done. I will try to see if I can assign one more developer to that side and get it done. I think Ashish can handle it. What do you say Ashish?"

"Yeah sure, Praveen...I will."

"But Praveen, I can manage that..." Ravi tried to interrupt, unable to digest the fact that his work is being assigned to some other developer. He feared if this will be used against him during the review cycle.

"No...I don't want to take chances this time, Ravi. After the meeting, Ashish will come to you and you have to tell him exactly what test cases are remaining and how they should be automated."

"Ok..." said Ravi trying to control his anger. 'At least Ashish could have had some sense in leaving that part to me. Now what can I do, I will unnecessarily lose credit for whatever I did till today.'

But what can Ashish do? It is after all a competitive world. He had to show himself in the best light to Praveen to prove that he is better than the rest. 'This is the way the world works.'

Carl spoke, "Yeah...if you need more resources then I think we can borrow someone from the test team. What do you say, Prashanth?"

Prashanth was the test lead. The project that Ravi was working on was one module of a supermarket related software solution being designed for some US-based supermarket chain. There were five developers in the module, one team lead, two testers, one test lead and one business analyst. One developer, Rajeev, was onsite who represented the client onsite. It was a medium-sized team as it was a critical component of the overall solution.

"No...I cannot spare any resources from my side. We are busy with our test case identification process and reviews. I am sorry."

Praveen spoke, "No problem, Carl. I will take care of this thing with the help of my developer resources."

'Yes, you are like a baba in some ashram. You grant anything that the client asks for. Why should you bother? Ultimately, it is me who will slog here. #$#@$#' cursed Ravi because that was the only thing he could ever do.

"Ok Praveen...then let's get to the bugs getting fixed on UI for its release. I see ten bugs on my screen here. How are we doing against the list?" said Carl.

Ravi picked up the thread, "I am done with 6 bugs. Will be finishing the remaining four bugs in two days...i.e., by Friday..."

"Ravi! You are done with only 6 bugs? I thought you said you will complete all the fixes by last Monday?" said Praveen.

'Damn it! Why should Praveen always poke me like this when the entire team is here? And that too when the test team, the analyst and the client are a part of the call... Why doesn't he show some sense and make sure that we talk about it in private?' thought Ravi and said, "I...I slipped a bit. Some of my time was lost as I had to train Naina."

"We will talk about it after the meeting," said Praveen and continued, "development wise I think we are on track, Carl. You need not worry. We will meet the Monday deadline."

"You lifted my spirits, Praveen. But in case there are any issues and we do not meet the Friday timeline for some of the features, then we may have to decide about cutting out some features. So, please update me about the status on Friday. Now let's go over to the test side. How are we doing on that front, Prashanth?"

"We are doing fine with our test cases. We already did a couple of review cycles between ourselves, will be doing a review of the test cases with the entire team today and will do another review on Friday."

'What! A test case review meeting! My God! How many meetings? That will be the third meeting today,' thought Ravi.

"Prashanth, can you include me in the test case review cycle on Friday. I would like to participate in that meeting."

"Sure Carl, I will send you an invite."

"Ok then...guys we seem to be doing great then. I thank you all for the effort you are putting into this project. Let us ship a solid product this time."

"Thanks Carl...the team is working very hard for the success of the project. I am sure it will be successful," said Prashanth.

"Will meet you guys on Friday. Don't forget to send me an email invitation. Bye."

And the teleconference was over.

Ravi looked at his watch, it showed 8:50. Slowly everyone was getting up and leaving the room. “Ravi, we should talk. Come to my room,” said Praveen.

Looking at his manager’s face, Ravi could make out that he wasn’t in a good mood. ‘It is going to be a heated meeting that will follow now. Oh God! How do I manage this situation?’ thought Ravi and followed Praveen to his room.

“Ravi, close the door.”

Ravi closed the door and waited for the session to begin.

“Why are you late today? I called you up at 6:15 and made sure that you had enough time to make it to the office? Still you have come late? Also, what is this attire? What are all those mud stains on your trousers?”

“The stains, they happened when I was coming to the office by an auto. I had to take the auto as the office bus that I was coming in was involved in an accident and the driver was taken to the police station.”

“What? Are you serious?”

“Yes, I am...”

Praveen could not believe his own ears and thought it to be another reason which was cooked up by Ravi to fool him.

“Ha! Another of your stories, huh!”

“No Praveen, you can ask the bus coordinator.”

“I will surely talk to him. But this is the third time that I saw you coming half an hour late to office in the last two weeks. So, what happened on those two occasions? Were there accidents?”

“No...but there was no urgent work, right...so I started a bit late from home on the previous two occasions.”

"See! That shows your carelessness. I wanted to warn you last week itself, but I thought you would correct yourself. But today's mistake is something which I cannot forgive."

'Praveen talks as if he is a judge in the court, cannot forgive my mistakes. What can he do other than screwing up my review?' thought Ravi and said, "Praveen...I will take anything that you say about the previous two occasions but today I did start on time, I took the office bus and still ended up late not because of my mistakes but because of the issues on which I had no control."

"Ok...leave that issue aside. What about the test cases and bug fixes? Only 25% done and 6 bugs fixed? I told you that we should hit 100% code complete (finish the coding phase) and 100% test complete (finish the testing phase) by Friday this week, right. I wouldn't want to see anyone working this weekend. Do you understand this point?"

"Yes, I do. I will try to achieve code complete by Friday but achieving 100% test complete by Friday might not be possible for me. I will work on the weekend and complete the tests by Monday."

"Why can't you do this by Friday? You should have prioritised your things well. Why did you slip on the tests?"

This discussion had irked Ravi a bit and he said, "Since you are pushing me so much I am telling you. My friends in the other teams are taking extra credit when they write test cases. Here in the name of some new development process, I am being 'made' to write tests and it is being shown as a compulsory work for which I cannot claim extra credit."

"So?"

"So...as there is already a test team I did not get interested in writing the tests."

Praveen's ego was hurt. He could not tolerate such behaviour from his reports, so he got into a preachy mode and started explaining to Ravi, in Praveen's own style, what a developer is responsible for. "What? You are not interested in writing tests? So you don't bother about quality? Since we are developers, quality should start with us. Unless you write tests properly, we cannot maintain quality. Do you understand that? Also, I assigned you those tests because you were free for two days last week," he said.

Ravi was also in no mood to relent and said, "The test team is using my code to build their tests. Why should I do their job? Do you babysit your neighbour's son if your neighbours are off to a vacation?"

Praveen was aghast by hearing Ravi's reaction and said, "What? What do you mean?"

In the heat of the moment, Ravi did not know what he was saying. He continued, "I mean, just because you have time you don't babysit your neighbour's children, right? You don't do it because you don't feel like doing it. The same is the case with me. I don't like writing those test cases and that is why I am not writing them."

Praveen had enough of the argument and said, "Whether you like it or not, in our project you should write tests." Also he did not like leaving Ravi without frightening him and continued, "Yesterday I went through the tests you wrote. The quality of the tests is very poor." Ravi had managed to poke Praveen hard and though it wasn't evident from Praveen's face, he was raging with anger.

At this very moment Ramnath, the project manager of Praveen, knocked on the door and opened it.

"Hi Praveen, I have something to discuss with you. Come to my cabin whenever you have time." And then he noticed the scornful look on both Ravi and Praveen's faces and asked them, "What guys? What are you discussing so seriously?"

"Ravi is saying that he is not interested in writing tests for his components," complained Praveen.

With a smile Ramnath said, "Ravi, these are what limit you from growing in the organisation, man! You should learn to be proactive."

Overwhelmed at this kind of response from the management, Ravi said, "It is not that I am not writing tests, I was a bit slow. I will try to wrap it up by Friday."

"Not 'try', you 'should'," said Praveen trying to show to his manager that he can push his team well.

"Ok guys. Bye...Praveen, don't forget the meeting I asked for. It is kind of urgent," saying this Ramnath closed the door.

"Ashish will come to your desk now. Distribute the tests between yourselves. See Ashish and learn something, Ravi. He is always proactive and ready to take up work which is not his."

"Ok..." Ravi was getting angry and bored with his lecture right in the morning.

"Also when you are in a call with the client, do not mention things like 'I still have four more bugs to do' etc. That kind of gives a bad impression about us. You should learn some basic communication strategies, Ravi. Go now."

Having listened to all that Praveen had to say, Ravi thought, 'For the last three years, there hasn't been a single manager who hadn't repeated the same words that Praveen is telling me today. Either the fault is with me or these managers are always like this. Since I know I am not faulty, the second conjecture that 'all managers are like this' is correct.'

❖❖❖

Chapter 4

Rendezvous with Silverlight

9:10 a.m.

Ravi came out of Praveen's cabin and closed the door. He felt relaxed. The worst he had feared for has happened and 'passed'. He smiled and thought, 'This is a common thing for me with Praveen. I am already done with all the bug fixes but did not mention so as he would have surely assigned some more work to me. At least I am safe for the time being.'

To clean the stains on his trousers, he went to the washroom. While cleaning the stains, the first name he remembered was 'Vijay'. 'All this happened because he took my bike today. #$@#@'. Then his thoughts went onto the way his manager dealt with him in the morning. To cheer himself he thought, 'I heard somewhere that it is difficult to deal with a nagging wife but my case is worse. These managers are worse than nagging wives. Damn! So, if I don't work on tests then that means I am destroying my career, is it...bullshit!'

Thinking like this, he went to his cubicle no. 4007. He was always proud of his cubicle number. It indicated 4th floor and cube no. '007'. 'James Bond,' he thought. 'I am the Bond of 4th floor. Just as James Bond kicks the asses of hooligans, so do I kick the asses of bugs. *Wah*! What a comparison...' He congratulated himself for coming up with such a great comparison between Bond and himself. Though Ravi might be a hero in killing bugs, still he wasn't as good as Bond was in flirting with girls. That was his only shortcoming.

Ravi was a James Bond fan. To reinforce the fact that his cube number is '007', he stuck some Bond posters to the walls of his cubicle. Apart from the Bond posters, there were a couple of Shahrukh Khan posters too. There was also a plaque in his cube which had some congratulatory message on it for successfully shipping some product. Other than that he had a computer at his disposal for doing his regular work.

Ravi's cubicle was opposite to Naina's and he noticed that Naina hadn't come to office yet. 'She skipped the meeting. Hope at least Praveen doesn't scold her...else I will have to rescue her,' he thought. Mentally preparing himself to confront Praveen and save Naina, he formulated certain strategies on how to counter Praveen if he questions Naina. After solidifying his strategy, he got back to his work.

He powered his box on. These days it is mandatory to switch off computers to save power. Recession had taken its toll on SOS too. There was no escaping the golden rule of cost cutting. SOS had already axed 200 people in the last six months and there were rumours that they were planning to lay off more people.

Though there were layoffs, some people were also being hired simultaneously. Two experienced resources from his team had been moved to other projects where there were some layoffs and two new members joined their team in the last one month. One was Naina and the other was Suresh. Naina was a fresher, just out of her college while Suresh had one year of experience. Naina had joined Ravi's team only last week, whereas Suresh had joined the team four weeks ago. There was also a rumour that people with greater than four years of experience were under the scanner as those resources cost high and the company was thinking about replacing such resources with less experienced freshmen who cost less.

Ravi did not know how much truth the rumour actually had but he tried to be a bit more careful with his work and avoid conflicts with his managers. But today it couldn't be avoided. 'This is too much. He is treating me like a slave. Why should I agree to whatever he says? I am working here for salary just like he does. Why should he force me into doing something which is not my work item,' he thought.

'Ctrl-Alt-Del'

He typed in his username and password and the PC took its own time to launch everything. The morning's meeting with Praveen had irritated Ravi badly. He was still cursing Praveen as he clicked on the Outlook button on the desktop to check his emails.

Inbox showed '15 new mails' and another folder for the 'SOS-Hyderabad' mails showed '63'.

He clicked on Inbox and eight of them were 'good morning' mails, a couple of mails were from SOS management informing of some organisational changes, three from the client making some requests, one reply from his manager and one mail from his teammate on some technical issue.

Having gone through a lengthy work-related discussion with Praveen, Ravi first opened the good morning mails. One of the mails was from his friend and colleague Naresh. It read...

If you forward this mail to ten other people, you will achieve success in whatever you do today. If you don't, you will never achieve what you want.

Good Morning.

Ravi hadn't expected to read this kind of crap right in the morning. He got up and shouted at Naresh.

"Naresh! What crap did you send me right in the morning?"

Naresh did not understand that statement. "What is this about?" he asked.

"That good morning mail you sent me. Why do you keep forwarding such stupid stuff? Why do you believe in it?"

Naresh laughed and said, "Hey! What do I have to lose by forwarding to ten other people, huh! So I just sent it off. Why should I bear the bad luck if it brings any? If you don't believe it, don't forward it to anyone."

Ravi had no answer to this and shouted, "Next time you send me such stuff I will kick your ass."

Naresh smiled and said, "Okay, next time we will see."

Ravi did not want to believe that mail. He wanted to delete it and forget about it. But simultaneously some other portion of his brain pricked him. 'Today you are going to take Naina out for a dinner. Why take chances? Forward it. What have you got to lose?'

The second argument sounded more logical and he quickly typed ten email ids in the 'To' list and forwarded the mail. He continued with the rest of the mails.

As soon as he finished reading the last 'good morning' mail, Ravi heard someone greet him and he turned to check who it was.

Ashish was standing beside him. He said, "Ravi, I wanted to ask you when I can come to you for the test case related thing that Praveen suggested in the morning."

"Hmm...let's schedule it at 3:00 p.m., that is, after lunch and meeting with the test team."

"I thought it might be a good idea if we can do it a bit early because I have just two days to finish this work. It will be great if we start now, otherwise I might not get the time."

"I understand your concern Ashish but Naina hasn't come in yet. We have a total of around 100 test cases to write and I am working on approximately 25 of them. Since Naina is working on the UI side, she said she will take around 50. It is a week since she is working on this thing. I haven't asked her how many she has finished. Let's wait till she comes, then we can distribute the stuff properly among ourselves. What say?"

Ravi actually wanted to work on his own work items for now and did not want to get into another meeting. But Ashish was not one who would leave so easily.

"Ravi, you are saying that you are writing 25 and she is working on 50. Since you know what the other 25 are, tell me what they are. I will work on them."

'God! Ashish is a leech,' thought Ravi and said, "Ok...let's go over the list then..."

Ravi took another 15 minutes explaining Ashish what the remaining test cases are and what test suite they had created till that point and how to use it. After the session, Ashish felt satisfied and he left saying that he will take the entire list of 25 remaining test cases while Ravi and Naina can look at their own portions.

Ravi thought... 'At least one burden is off my head now.' Ravi had already completed all his bug fixes but did not tick them off the bug tracker fearing more work. He only had the review screen to work on. 'I just have a day's work left. With Ashish shouldering the burden of coding the remaining test cases, I am comfortably placed for the Friday.'

But poor Ravi can manage things only to an extent. He cannot change the course of what is going to happen next.

He looked at the clock and it showed 9:30.

He got back to his machine and once again started checking his mails. He deleted the organisational change related mails as they were huge. 'If there is anything important, Praveen will tell us. Why waste my time on these,' thought Ravi and then moved over to those which were of immediate concern.

The first mail from the client had something to do with the machine upgrades that they were planning to do and the impact it would have on the project. The mail also stated some new requirements.

'These people plan for upgrades at such a late stage in the project and expect us to finish everything overnight #$#@! Now what is this request for new requirements with just two days to go? Let me see what Praveen has written in his reply to this mail. I pray that he doesn't commit himself to all these changes.'

He opened the mail from Praveen and his head started spinning. The mail read as follows...

Hi Carl and Rajeev,

We discussed thoroughly the changes that were requested by you. Based on our analysis, we think that it is possible for us to do a full test pass by Monday with those changes. The only thing that concerns us is the requirement about using the new Silverlight framework. We have only provided ASPX controls till now. We agree with you on the point that adding Silverlight controls to our UI adds significant value to the UI. I will discuss this with Ravi and send you an update by tonight. I think we should be able to do this by Friday next week. The only issue with Friday is that we might have to make modifications to our schedule.

Regards,

Praveen

"Silverlight!!!" Ravi felt as if a bolt of lightning struck him down. His heart sank to the lowest depths of Mariana trench (maybe even lower). 'Silverlight? In a week? Whom did Praveen discuss with and how come 'he' decided that it is possible? I don't have any experience with Silverlight and neither does Naina nor does anyone else in the team. How the hell did he deem it is possible?' Then he saw the next mail from Carl which was a reply to Praveen's mail and it read...

Hi Praveen,

That is awesome. But if you think we cannot make it by Monday, let us not get to the point of modifying our schedules. Let us take this feature in the next release.

Regards,

Carl

Ravi's mind settled down a bit and his senses returned to him. 'Thank God! Carl saved me. Otherwise I would have to sweat it out the next week to get these Silverlight controls in. But who in the first place actually discussed with Praveen and made the decision that it is possible for us to do this in one week.' Thinking this way, he proceeded to the last unread mail which was from Suresh, the new joiner. That mail was sent late in the night at 1:00 a.m. and was directly addressed to Praveen and CC'ed to the other developers. It was a complete surprise to Ravi. It read...

Hi,

I was debugging the UI component and I found that certain improvements could be made. I removed some sections from the UI code base which I thought were unnecessarily slowing down the UI rendering. I also made some tweaks to the underlying architecture and modified some classes. I want you to confirm whether these changes can be submitted to the stable branch.

Suresh

Ravi's irritation reached new levels. 'Modified the architecture? What kind of a joke is this? We have a deadline on Friday and he is talking about code changes at this stage? Also as far as I know there were not many issues that we noticed with our current code base. I don't understand why Suresh had to modify those sections.

Let me see how much Praveen gets convinced about this.' Not in a mood to fight with Suresh, Ravi thought of concentrating on his work for the time being. He deleted all the mails in that 'SOS-Hyderabad' folder as it was a discussion list full of random discussions about house rents, vehicle sales, general banter etc.

He opened his project and then started writing some code and debugging certain scenarios. He had been coding for a while when he heard someone say, "Hi Ravi..."

He turned to his left and saw Naina seated at her desk. She had come to the office just now.

'She is very late,' thought Ravi and checked his watch. It showed '9:56 a.m'.

"Hi Naina, you are late. You did not attend the meeting in the morning."

"Yeah...what happened you know? I was coming on my Honda Activa when the front tyre got punctured some two kilometres from my home, so I walked all the way back with my bike. It was already 8 by the time I reached home. Then I thought since I am already late, why not get this thing patched up and then come to office. Why? Did anyone ask for me?"

"No...even I was a bit late. Nothing of great importance was discussed in the meeting."

"Oh, okay...I was actually afraid that someone might have said something about me in the meeting because I was late."

At the same moment, Ravi heard Praveen shout to his team, "Anyone coming for breakfast?"

Ravi checked his watch and it was '10 a.m'.

❖❖❖

Chapter 5

Praveen's Revenge

10:00 a.m.

As most of the members had arrived early for the meeting, all of them were ready for the breakfast. Ravi was a bit surprised to see that Praveen hadn't spoken to Naina yet.

'He gave me a lecture for 15 minutes because I was late? He seems to have ignored the fact that Naina also walked in very late. Anyway good that he did not raise this issue, otherwise I will have to think about how to save her,' thought Ravi and followed his team to the cafeteria.

The team was near the entrance to the cafeteria. Praveen had just finished a small conversation with Ravi on some UI related fixes and was standing beside him when Ravi heard someone say hello to him

"Hello Ravi..." He turned around and saw that it was his friend Pradeep who was working on another project.

"Hey...hi Pradeep...how are you doing? Long time, no see..."

"Yeah, long time...I am doing well. How are you? Last time I met you, you were complaining about your manager, right. Is he still bothering you?" saying this Pradeep laughed loudly.

Praveen stopped for a moment and stared at both Ravi and Pradeep and then continued walking with the team.

Ravi was stunned for a moment. He did not know what to say and tried to cover it up. He started talking loudly so that Praveen could hear the conversation, "Uh...actually that was last year. Now I have a great manager, you know. Understands our needs very well...by the way I have come with my team today. Will talk to you later...bye..."

Pradeep was surprised because he had met Ravi only two months back and that was when he heard Ravi complaining about his manager. Confused with that statement from Ravi, Pradeep tried to continue, "Oh! Is it...but it was only two months ago that..." and stopped after looking at Ravi who was making some weird signs which confused him more.

Ravi was standing with his back towards Praveen, who had stopped again to listen to the conversation between them. Ravi was trying his best to convey the message to Pradeep that it was not the time to discuss the matter. Finally looking at that pitiable expression on Ravi's face, Pradeep understood that the discussion was troubling Ravi.

"Ok, bye then. Will meet you during lunchtime..."

Ravi was on the verge of kicking Pradeep if he continued for some more time. So hearing the last statement from Pradeep made him feel relieved, he put up a big smile on his face and said, "Bye."

'Phew! That was a close shave. At least I could manage something. Next time I complain to someone about my manager, I should make sure that I show them his photograph.' Thinking this way Ravi started walking briskly to join Praveen and his team.

After giving the orders and receiving their items, the team sat down to have breakfast.

'That person, Pradeep or whoever he was, was definitely talking about me. Ravi is covering things up. Next review cycle, I will show him what I am capable of doing. Why...wait...why wait till next review cycle? I can screw things up for him right now. I will make him run on that Silverlight requirement.' Thinking this way Praveen called, "Ravi..."

"Yes...Praveen."

"You understand that Silverlight requirement from Carl, right?"

Ravi thought, 'I have just now started eating my *dosa* and there is a technical discussion again. I am getting tired of this thing. Why do these people keep talking about work during these breaks?' He said, "Yes Praveen...I understood that mail."

"Good...can you verify by tonight as to what changes we need to make for this component?"

"Tonight?"

"Yes, tonight. Carl mentioned in his mail that we should do it for the next release, right. I was thinking that if we can start Silverlight on Monday, then we can finish it as the first item for our next release."

Ashish said, "Yeah, looks like a good idea."

Ravi gulped and felt as if a big chunk of stone was thrust down his throat. In a weak tone, he asked, "Oh! When do you think we should complete coding for Silverlight?"

"Since the request is to replace our existing components with Silverlight, I am thinking that it should take us two weeks. What do you think?" said Praveen.

"Two weeks!" Ravi was shocked. "But why are we in such a hurry, Praveen?"

"See, we don't know what exactly we will be doing for our next release. So if we finish off this thing early, we can concentrate on other items coming to us. Let's wrap up this feature first. I am scheduling a meeting at 12:00. Let us talk more about it in the meeting. I will provide you with the necessary help on Silverlight."

After finishing his statement, Praveen felt satisfied that he had proven his might to Ravi. 'Idiot! Thinks that he can talk anything behind my back? Now this should settle him for another two weeks.'

Ravi was shocked because of two reasons. One because he was being forced to work on Silverlight and two because Praveen said 'Meeting!' Ravi was already troubled with the thought of attending the meeting with the test team in the afternoon. 'The test team scheduled for another meeting in the afternoon...God! Will this tirade never end...' thought Ravi. He did not feel like sitting there for more time and checked his watch. It showed 10:15.

Everyone was done with the breakfast by around 10:25. As the group started walking towards the lifts to go to the fourth floor, Suresh approached Ravi and asked, "Ravi...did you see my mail? I wanted to talk to you about the changes I did to the UI. When can we meet?"

Not in a mood to encounter another meeting, Ravi gave his standard reply, "Let's meet at 3 o'clock, that is, after the meeting with the test team."

As usual Suresh protested, "No...it is a very small thing. It will take us only 15 minutes. Can we do it quickly?"

"No, Suresh...I have lots of work to do. Most of my time in the morning got wasted in meetings. Let's do it only in the afternoon."

"I will tell you about the changes very quickly. It will not take much time," Suresh pleaded.

Ravi improvised over his last excuse, "No...I am in the middle of a code change and I will forget the sequence if I have a discussion with you. So, let's meet at 3:00 p.m."

Having no other option, Suresh agreed to Ravi's proposal. But he thought, "I will raise this issue in the 'scrum' (a daily meeting in the morning where the entire team assembles and each person updates the team about what he/she did the previous day, what they are going to do today and whom or what they are blocked on. It is one of the components of the 'Agile methodology' of product development. The meeting is supposed to go for around 15 minutes). I will make sure that the whole team recognises my effort."

Ding!

The lift arrived at the ground floor and everyone boarded it.

❖❖❖

Chapter 6

Scrum Time

10:30 a.m.

Ding!

The lift arrived on the fourth floor. After everyone got off the lift, Praveen declared that it was 'scrum time'. Praveen went off to the cubicles to get the business analyst and the test team to assemble for the scrum.

Scrum. This word is a major irritant to many software engineers.

Ravi was thinking, 'Scrum...#$%#@! We already did a status update in the meeting with the client. Now why this scrum again? Also this word scrum rhymes with scum. What a coincidence!'

The entire team assembled in the area between the cubicles and business analyst Sudeep was chosen as the 'scrum master' (one who drives the meeting) for the day.

The first chance went to Ashish. "Hmm...yesterday I completed the unit tests for our services, worked on automating some sequences. Today I talked to Ravi and took the list of tests that I would be working on."

Praveen was happy with the update from Ashish. 'He is my star developer,' he thought and said, "Yesterday I worked on writing some scripts and participated in some discussions with our management team and customers."

It was Charan's turn. Charan was a senior tester in the team. He said, "I completed my test case enumeration and participated in an internal test review meeting yesterday. Also I tested the new

UI which Ravi shared with me and I raised a new bug in it."

Till that moment Ravi was lost in his own world and was thinking about the discussion that happened around Silverlight. He was deeply thinking about what changes he will have to make for that thing to work, when the words 'Ravi' and 'new bug' brought him back to this world.

"What?"

"I raised a new bug on your name."

Praveen said, "What Ravi you haven't looked at your bug list today?"

"I...I...no...I...was working on the review screen and hadn't checked the updated list."

"Learn to be more active man! Anyway how big is the issue, Charan?"

"I don't know. When we use our UI and write a mail and click the send button..."

At this point, Ravi interrupted, "It works fine. I checked this portion properly."

"Yeah, the send email feature works as it is, but after clicking the send button when someone wants to cancel it immediately that is not happening."

"What?"

"Yes, I clicked on the 'Send' button and then immediately clicked on the 'Cancel' button and I still received the mail."

"Is this a bug?" Ravi was seething with anger.

"That is a good suggestion, Charan," chipped in Sudeep.

"But is that a proper scenario, Sudeep? The user clicks on the

'Send' button only when he is finished with writing his mail, right? What is this thing about clicking on 'Cancel' immediately?"

"That case is valid because if the user clicks on 'Send' by mistake and then immediately realises his mistake and tries to cancel it, we should support that scenario..." said Praveen.

"But how would we handle this? By the time someone clicks on 'Cancel', the program would already be executing the 'Send' function. How do I cancel that action? I don't think even Outlook or Gmail has such a feature."

"You are looking only at the problem, Ravi. The solution is simple, use threading there," Praveen started explaining how to handle this scenario. He talked at length for five minutes and after making sure that he had driven the point well, he concluded his speech by saying, "It is simple?"

After listening to the speech, Sudeep spoke first. He said, "You get awesome ideas, Praveen. You are a genius!"

'Awesome idea...my foot...I have to implement threading now in that module for some useless scenario,' thought Ravi. He was not going to accept the change so easily. "Threading takes time and that function is already complicated. Also I will have to write new tests for the same, I may not be able to do all this by Friday."

Praveen argued, "Why should it take time? It is just modifying two functions and five tests, right? You may have to add two more test cases. Is that not so?"

"Yes..."

"Then all that is just a couple of hours of work, right. Why should it take time?" Praveen repeated his argument.

Put so superficially, it looked like a coherent argument. Ravi and everyone in the team nodded in agreement. But Ravi knew that superficially everything looks simple. Once you get into the implementation, this thing will drag on at least for a day. He knew that it was useless to argue with Praveen. Praveen had his way when it came to things like these.

Unable to counter his manager's argument, Ravi finally agreed, "Okay...I will try to implement threading then." He thought, 'I know why Charan brought up this issue now. He is definitely taking his revenge on me.'

There is a long story between Ravi and Charan. Once upon a time they were friends. But it so happened that a year ago, when both of them were working on the same project, Ravi showed some over-enthusiasm because of which Charan suffered.

'...the tests are buggy. There is no problem with my code. I went through his test cases and found those issues. They need to be resolved before those test cases can be used...' this was a portion from the mail that Ravi sent to his superiors informing them about the status of testing. The repercussions were bad and Charan was shown this exact mail as one of the reasons for denying him a promotion. From that day on, Charan had been purposefully pushing Ravi into problematic situations whenever he could. Charan always scanned Ravi's code with X-ray precision. Today's report was again one such act of revenge.

Raghu who was another tester in the team gave his report. Ravi, Prashanth, Sudeep and Naresh followed him. When it came to Suresh, he delivered Ravi another shock.

"I implemented some test cases and fixed some database bugs. Finally I went through the UI code base and found some issues. I wrote a mail about it to the development team. Still haven't got any updates on this issue."

"As far as I know, there are no issues with the UI code base,"

Ravi tried to defend his code.

"No, I found some. For example, the lady's image on the first screen wasn't to my liking, so I changed it."

"What? That image was given to me by Sudeep. How can you change it?"

"I did not find her attractive."

"No, Suresh. We decided on that image after discussing with our customers," said Sudeep.

"I don't know. That lady who is shown pushing the cart has a kid in her arm and it looks like we are targeting the family audience. I changed it to a trendier one where a boy and girl are shown shopping together," he was still blabbering something when Praveen interrupted him.

"No...it has already been decided. Let's keep it that way. If there are any more changes discuss them with Ravi and he will tell you what was done according to the specification." Praveen had the final word and the matter was settled for the day.

Ravi thought, 'Why me? I already have a lot of work to do. These meetings are really killing my time.'

"Ok..." Suresh sounded a bit disappointed because his hard work did not get good recognition today. But he was not someone who would give up so easily. He thought, 'What if these people think I am not correct? I will try chatting with Rajeev or Carl today and decide what the image is.'

It was Naina's turn. "I had around 50 test cases to write for UI. I could complete only 5 as I wasn't well aware of all the functions and classes. I have been trying hard but could only manage this much."

Ravi received a jolt. Only 5 done and 45 remaining, 'That

means I have to share some work. Why are all releases like this? Just before the deadline, new work gets assigned and old work piles up.' Thinking this way, Ravi managed to speak before Praveen could.

"I will take up 20 of your tests and complete them. After this meeting show me what you have completed till today and I will proceed from there." After saying this Ravi thought, 'Now Praveen cannot complain about anything. I have successfully managed to show him that I can manage stuff,' and smiled at Praveen.

But Ravi was wrong again. "Ravi...Naina has been here for around a week now and you have been helping her all the time, right?"

"Yes."

"But even after that she has finished only 5? So, is that not your fault?"

Ravi missed the point completely. It was his responsibility to get Naina ramped up and her rate of completion showed it as a black spot on Ravi's capabilities. But Ravi could not accept that and at the same time could not dare to utter anything that hurt Naina. He was in a fix.

'What should I say now? Even if I try to defend myself, Praveen will not agree. Defending myself would mean putting the blame on Naina. Better I accept it as my mistake.' Thinking this way, he said, "Praveen, actually I am spending time with her on a daily basis. We have covered many portions of the code base till now. But since the code base is big and the test suite that I developed is also big, it is confusing for anyone to understand all the flows in just a week. We will complete this knowledge acquisition in maybe another week. Meanwhile, I will try to complete as many tests as possible from those pending 45."

Praveen was still not convinced but was at least satisfied that someone owned up to do the remaining work and said, "Okay... but see to it that you complete all this by Friday. Naina, you too get this knowledge acquisition done as soon as possible. We have new work coming our way after Monday, so you should be ready by then."

"Sure Praveen, I will," replied Naina.

Anxious to know what that the new work was, Ravi asked, "What is this new work?"

"The new Silverlight controls that Carl was asking us to do."

Ravi felt depressed whenever Praveen mentioned Silverlight to him. It reminded him of more work of which he perceived no noticeable value. So in a very weak tone, he said, "Okay..."

"Anyway let's discuss more about it in the 12:00 o'clock meeting," said Praveen and closed the discussion.

Just then someone brought the issue of managing some other scenarios if the team provided Silverlight controls. A minor discussion followed between the team members and the meeting dragged on for another ten minutes. The discussion was open-ended and resulted in nothing concrete.

'What a waste of time! I have to complete my work...' thought Ravi and he was getting restless.

Finally, the scrum ended at 10:55 and Ravi heaved a sigh of relief.

❖❖❖

Chapter 7

A Twist in the Tale

10:55 a.m.

"Naina, let's go over your test cases and see what I should take up."

Naina opened the test list viewer and said, "This is the complete list of test cases that I had been working on. I did these..." and she marked the test cases that she had finished and showed him what were still remaining.

"Okay...so you have finished five and are working on three more now. Great! For now, I will take those 10 and will try to complete them by evening." Saying this Ravi got back to his desk, opened the editor and started where he had left his work before he left for the breakfast.

Ravi worked for 10 minutes when he noticed Naina getting up and going somewhere.

Anxious to know where she was going, Ravi asked her, "Where are you going, Naina?"

"Praveen sent an email to me asking me to come to his cabin."

"What is it about? Any UI related discussion?"

"No...I think he wants to talk to me about why I came late to office today. The mail said it was something to do with the meeting that happened in the morning."

Ravi thought, 'Praveen is definitely going to say something or the other. It is the correct time for me to fall into Naina's good books.' So he said, "Naina, Praveen generally gets serious when we come late to office. Today morning, he gave me a big lecture for coming late. Why I am telling you this is because you need not be bothered about whatever he says there. It is a common thing for all of us."

Naina became a bit tensed and said, "Oh! Do you think he is going to scold me?"

"Maybe yes...the chances are a bit high. Just listen to whatever he says and do not bother about his statements. He is like that..."

"Okay...let me go to his room and see what he tells me," Naina was visibly upset with whatever information Ravi gave her. Noticing this Ravi assured her again, "Don't worry, Naina. Just forget whatever he says, everything will be alright." He looked at her as she went into Praveen's room.

Ravi was busy coding a test case but at the same time maintained a watch on Praveen's cabin. At around 11:15, he noticed the door of Praveen's cabin open and Naina come out. 'If Praveen had used his talent, she would be on the verge of crying now. Good time for me to console her and gain a good impression.'

Ravi noticed that she was going towards the water filter and decided to meet her there. He got up from his seat and raced towards her. By the time Ravi caught up with her, she was at the filter filling her glass.

He was surprised to note that she looked fine and seemed to have had a normal conversation with Praveen. "So how did your meeting with Praveen go," Ravi enquired.

"Went well...he just called me to know how I am progressing with my work. Wanted to know what I am working on today and whether I have any work tonight."

Ravi was even more surprised because Praveen didn't seem

to have asked her the reason for her coming late. “Did he say something for coming late today?”

“Yeah...he asked me about that and I told him my reason. He told me that he lives somewhere near my place and that I should have called him. He said he could pick me up anytime. He never sounded angry throughout the discussion,” said Naina with a smile.

It was purely a new experience for Ravi because he had never seen his manager behave so coolly with any other report. “Oh! Is it?” said Ravi. ‘There is something fishy going on here. He did not scold her and on top of that offered to give her a lift? Also asked her whether she has any work tonight? Strange!’ thought Ravi.

Probing the issue further, he asked, “You said, he asked you whether you were free tonight or not, right? Why did he ask you that question?”

“Oh that thing...actually he said that since I am new to Hyderabad, he could take me around the city and we could have dinner at the Taj Residency. But I told him that you had asked me out for a dinner today.”

“Oh! Is it? What did he say for that?”

“He said, in case you cannot take her out tonight I could call him and he will take me along.” This statement made Ravi think harder.

Ravi filled his glass and both of them started walking towards their cubicles. “Since we are talking about dinner, yesterday you said that you will tell me whether it is possible for you to come with me for the dinner tonight, right?” asked Ravi.

“Yes...I am working on those test cases. Apart from that I don’t have any other work. Have to see if any of that Silverlight work comes to me.”

"Leave the test cases to me. I don't think you can work on more than ten in the next two days. I will complete as many as possible. So, that means you are free for the dinner, right?" Ravi said with a broad grin on his face.

"In that case, I think I can come for the dinner. By the way, is anyone else joining us for the dinner?"

The question took Ravi by surprise. He cooked up an answer on the fly. "Actually I asked Ashish, Naresh and Priya who is another friend of mine. They agreed but I don't know how many of them will turn up in the evening."

"Cool. That is the main reason why I told Praveen that I am going out with you. It is always fun to go out with more people, you know. It would be boring to just go out with him for sightseeing."

"I will know by five in the evening as to who is coming with us." Ravi thought, 'This is a tricky situation. Should I call others or shouldn't I?'

Talking this way, they reached their cubicles and both of them got back to their work. But Ravi couldn't concentrate on his work. The new development that Naina had talked about was unsettling him. 'Why is Praveen suddenly interested in taking Naina around? He is not scolding her...hmm...what could be the reason?'

Suddenly he remembered something which gave him a good hint about why Praveen was behaving this way with Naina. The day after Naina joined the project, Praveen presented her with a box of chocolates. 'Just wanted to congratulate you for getting selected to our project' was the reason that Praveen gave her. But Ravi and Naresh discussed at length about what the possible motives could be.

He remembered Naresh saying, 'He never gifted us anything. Why this sudden change in behaviour?' Even after racking their brains for an hour, they couldn't arrive at any plausible conclusion.

This Monday Naresh and Ravi were surprised to find another box of chocolates on Naina's desk. On investigating about the box, they found that Praveen had gifted it to her. This time the reason was that one of his relatives brought that from US.

Naresh and Ravi discussed the issue again and this time Naresh came up with an explanation. "Praveen is 31 and is still unmarried. He is just five years elder to us and is an eligible bachelor. I think Praveen is trying to woo Naina. There can be no other explanation to this," he said.

But Ravi did not agree. He struck off that argument by saying, "Did you ever see his face properly? Did you ever notice any trace of an emotion such as humour or love on it? That fellow is too committed to work, dude. He is not capable enough of even thinking on those lines. Also with half his hair already gone, do you think Naina will fall for him?" saying this Ravi started laughing.

But today, with the way things were going on, Ravi finally concluded that Naresh was correct. But this thought had increased his heartbeat. 'Now Praveen knows that I am competing with him...how do I tackle this situation and win Naina's hand?'

Having unearthed such a great find, Ravi found it difficult to concentrate on his work. 'What the hell! Competition from my own manager! Man! Never imagined I would face such a situation.' But he was happy that Naina had chosen him over his older competitor for the dinner. That fact made him feel a bit elated too.

But at the same time a new thought cropped up. 'What if Praveen tries to break the relation between me and Naina? What if he makes me a fool in front of her? Praveen is a crooked ass. I am sure he will not leave this issue so lightly,' thought Ravi.

With these thoughts, Ravi's mind started heating up. Ravi got into an explosive mood and thought, 'If he is my manager, it is only for the office work. I don't need to behave as if I am his slave. This place will explode if he tries to meddle with my affairs. I will show him what I am. I am ready for the fight...'

❖❖❖

Chapter 8

A Valuable Lesson

11:30 a.m.

Having decided what he should do with Praveen, Ravi got back to his work. He was lost in his world of programming for around ten minutes, when he felt a hand on his shoulder. He was startled by this and turned fast to see who it was.

"Hi Ravi..." it was his friend Rahul.

"Uh...hey...hi Rahul. So...what's up man? How are you doing?"

"Can we go out for a cup of coffee? I have something to tell you. This is not the place for that."

Ravi was busy with a lot of work but Rahul was also one of his best friends so he did not deny his request. Ravi did not understand anything. 'What can such an issue be that he doesn't want to discuss when everyone is around? Anyway he is going to tell me, so why break my head on this.' Thinking this he followed Rahul to the corridor.

"Listen Ravi...I don't want you to discuss this thing with anyone."

"What thing?"

"What I am going to tell you now."

"Ok...I will not tell anyone."

"I am resigning from my job today."

Ravi was surprised, "You got a better offer elsewhere?"

"No...I was actually asked to leave and so I resigned."

Ravi was shocked. Rahul had almost three years of experience and was a candidate with a good skill set. 'So, recession has hit Rahul's project too? How long is this situation going to continue?' Thinking this way, Ravi asked, "Is it due to recession? Are they reducing the head count because of some cash crunch?"

"No my story is not linked to recession. It is basically because of a clash between me and my manager."

"Oh! What did you do?"

"I did not do anything. Six months ago, I asked my manager to consider me for an on-site opportunity. He promised me that my name would be considered first if an opportunity comes up."

"Then?"

"Two months later, I came to know from my friend that our client in UK requested for a resource. I immediately went to my manager and asked him to consider me for it. Even at that time, he told me that I am the most capable person in the project and that I would surely be considered for it. But fifteen days later, we got the information that another teammate of ours was chosen for that position."

"Oh!"

"I went to my manager and asked him how someone else was chosen when he had promised to consider my name for it. He started giving me some dumb reasons that the position had to be filled quickly and since I did not have the visa and stuff ready, they chose the other person for it who had a visa."

"What did you do then?"

"I knew that visa wasn't the problem and I argued with him.

He finally admitted that apart from visa processing, he also thought that I wasn't ready for the position yet."

"Oh! If that was the case he could have told you that in the beginning, right? Why did he have to hide this from you?"

"Correct! I asked him the same question and also as to what additional criteria was used to select that candidate over me."

"What did he say?"

"He said it seems that the other candidate is more proactive with customer issues than you are. I asked my manager to cite some examples and he could not show any. Man! Everything is based on perception and relations, you know. That candidate who was selected was always around my manager and he maintained a good relation with him and that was the main reason my manager selected him."

Ravi was surprised with the explanation. "What! But I thought merit was more important than the relations."

"Merit...I forgot that word a couple of years ago, dude. Here there is nothing called merit or ethics or decency. My manager always promised me that I will be the first one to be considered for the opportunity and now someone else is selected. And we are regularly taught corporate rules here. Huh! Such a joke..."

"So far there was no issue, right. What happened after that?" Ravi enquired.

"I got irritated with his statement that the other person was more proactive than me. I commented that my manager selected him because the other person was his friend."

"Oh!"

"My manager opposed it and made more statements about me. He started pricking me on various other issues. He started saying that I don't maintain quality in my code and that I don't concentrate on testing my code etc. You noticed that change in attitude? All the while he had been saying that I do great work and now he immediately finds lots of issues with my work. He also mentioned that I take time in understanding the specification before I work on the design."

"What? He doesn't want you to understand the specification before the design?"

"No...he was saying that I take two to three days to understand the whole thing and only then work on the design. But there are others, it seems, who understand the specification in a day and immediately give him the design the next day. That quality is appreciated by clients is what he told me."

"Oh! Is that true?"

"You know what? I always explained the requirements to that fellow who was selected. I know for sure that I am more eligible than him."

"Ok...that means your manager was telling you random stories."

"Yes...instead of trying to accept the fact that he messed up things, he was trying to put the blame on me. He tried hard to show me that I was not fit for that position. I tried to defend my position by saying that I was a merit student in college and also had great track record at SOS over the last few years. But he did not listen to any of it and started saying random stuff that academic record and success in a couple of projects doesn't necessarily mean I am a capable person."

"What does he want then?"

"It seems, I joined his team only eight months ago and he wanted to evaluate me for another year and only then decide whether I would suit for better positions in the project. He started telling me how hard he worked and grew in the organisation etc., and started coaching me on how trivial issues like these shouldn't bother me. This irritated me further and I made some remarks which ruptured our relation."

"What did you say?"

"I noticed on many occasions that my manager sleeps in his cabin after lunch. Whenever I get into his cabin I notice that he is dozing off. I knock on the door and he wakes up with a start, gropes for his mouse and starts moving it on the table in a fuzzy manner to fool me into believing that he was awake."

"So? How is that related to this incident?" enquired Ravi.

Rahul got furious, "Wait...don't interrupt me when I am still narrating the incident. I am getting to the same point. When my manager started boasting about his hardworking nature and how I should emulate him, I told him that when he, who regularly dozes off in office can become a manager I am fit for any position."

'What guts!' Ravi thought. "Dude that was very brave of you. What happened after that?"

"That statement led to a heated discussion between us and I think I shouted some expletives at him in anger. I think I used something like the 'F' word. It put me on the defensive when my manager complained about my behaviour to the management. Also since he is the manager, his managers gave more value to what he said compared to what I had to say."

It was a complete surprise for Ravi. He thought, 'Oh! I never thought from that angle. It is easy for my manager to attack me. He will have bigger and better contacts here than I do.' Thinking this Ravi said, "So, your manager took revenge on you?"

"Yes...my manager used this incident as a major point against me in the reviews that happened a month ago. He gave me the lowest possible rating and defended his case with specific examples which showed me in bad light. Now you tell me dude, while working on a project we all commit mistakes, right?"

"Yeah...right..."

"These managers take advantage of all these incidents at specific moments like these. He generalised my behaviour by linking the fight that I had with him to another incident with our client. That was a very minor issue where I told the client that I am not going to work on a specific feature because of some constraints. He successfully convinced the management that I lack communication skills and that I fight with clients."

"Oh!"

"My review got totally screwed up and I was given the option of either getting fired or resign from the company voluntarily. To avoid a black spot on my resume, I opted for the latter."

"Dude! You screwed up things badly. You should have apologised to your manager right in the beginning. I think things would have settled down then and there itself."

"Apology? To that idiot! Never! He is an untrustworthy individual and I don't care about him anymore." Rahul was visibly angry with his boss for whatever had happened. He then cooled down a bit and said, "Listen Ravi, once you have done something like scolding your boss or irritating him beyond a point, no amount of apology heals that wound. Now that I have crossed that threshold I know what the result is."

"So, have you got any other offer yet? It is recession time, right? Any success?"

"I have an interview this week with Signex software solutions and I am preparing a bit...just called you aside to tell you how

SOS treated me for working hard for them. I will not be in office from tomorrow."

Here Ravi differed with Rahul. He said, "I don't think you can put the blame on the company for the actions of certain individuals. They aren't the company, right."

"You are talking from an idealistic point of view. For us, our managers represent the company. They did not treat me well and that automatically means SOS did not treat me well."

"Yeah, maybe. Anyway good luck for your interviews, dude. You will definitely make it."

"Thanks for the wishes, dude. How are things going in your life?"

"Me! I am bogged down with lots of work, dude. My manager is dumping work on my head on a regular basis. There is another meeting at 12 o'clock where he said he will tell me how I can add more features in five working days."

"Managers are crazy. They make us work like donkeys and then screw up our reviews. I hate them."

Ravi joked on this aspect, "Maybe when we become managers we should try to be better people."

Rahul laughed and said, "Yeah...we should try to be better managers in future."

Ravi looked at his watch and it showed 11:45...

"Rahul...I have lots of work to do."

"Ok. No problem...let's go," saying this they cut their discussion and walked towards their respective cubicles.

Ravi thought that his chat with Rahul was a God sent message. It was an eye opener for him. 'Good that I came to know about what would happen if I pick up a fight with Praveen.' He now started feeling bad for having fought with his manager in the morning. 'I have unnecessarily fought with him in the morning,' he thought. 'But, anyway I cannot do anything about it now. In future, I should be careful. I should try to use other intelligent ways to thwart his attacks. But how?' he thought. But that last question was a difficult one to answer.

'Anyway, right now things are taking place in good order. Praveen seems to have forgotten about the fight that I had with him in the morning. Naina has agreed to come with me to the dinner. Let me think about Praveen only when he really creates a problem,' thought Ravi and continued with his work.

❖❖❖

Chapter 9

Exceeding Expections

11:55 a.m.

It was just a few minutes ago that Ravi started his work, when his internal office chat messenger popped up a chat window.

The message was from Praveen, "Guys! Assemble in my room in 5 minutes. We shall do a small review of our progress and also discuss the changes that we should be ready within the next two weeks."

Despite knowing the fact that he had to attend a meeting at 12:00, Ravi could not stop himself from venting his anger at the thought of another meeting. 'This is it. This is the limit. I haven't got a chance to work continuously for at least an hour. Meetings, meetings and more meetings... This way, I will have to stay late and do my job... $#@$##... Hope I don't have to forgo the dinner with Naina.'

Ravi typed the reply, "Coming." Grudgingly Ravi got up from his desk and walked towards Praveen's room. He opened the door and found that there were three chairs in the cabin which were taken up by Praveen, Naresh and Naina. Suresh and Ashish stood near the wall and so Ravi sat on the table.

Praveen turned towards his computer and opened a document which contained the items that were to be completed for the release. He took a red marker and copied that list onto the whiteboard. Feeling proud of his own work, Praveen now turned around to face his team.

"Team, this is the list that we need to complete for the release. Is there anything that I missed from noting down here?"

“Yeah...you have not listed down the deployment and integration scripts that I am working on,” answered Ashish.

“Oh...yes...you are right,” saying this Praveen copied that item onto the board and asked, “anything else?”

Everyone was thinking hard to check if there was anything else that was missing from the points listed down the board. Nothing special hit their heads. Seeing that everyone was silent Praveen said, “Ok...that means we can proceed then.”

One of the items on the board read ‘Silverlight controls for UI’. That item on the board was a shocker. Seeing that point on the board Ravi was seething with anger. ‘What the hell? Why did he include it as an item for this release?’

Meanwhile, Praveen marked who owned what against each point. He started from point number one and started asking the corresponding owner for the status. He skipped ‘Silverlight’ and covered all the other points. Everything looked to be ‘on track’ and Praveen was satisfied with his team’s progress.

“So, looks like we are doing fine for Friday. Now I will discuss about this new Silverlight requirement with Ravi, if anyone else is interested you can stay back else you can leave.”

Naina stayed back as she was working on UI and Ashish stayed back because of his enthusiasm to contribute to every bit of the project.

‘Why is Ashish staying back? He is unnecessarily meddling with my part of the project,’ thinking this way, Ravi turned towards Ashish and putting up a smile on his face said, “Ashish did you work with Silverlight anytime?”

“No. Do you have any experience or any idea?”

“No...what about you, Naina?”

"Same here. No experience with Silverlight," giggled Naina.

Meanwhile, Ravi noticed that Praveen was busy searching for something.

Eager to know what Praveen was searching for, Ravi asked, "What are you searching for, Praveen?"

"A book, I had put it in my cupboard. Ah! There it is..." and he pulled out a four hundred page book. The title of the book read 'Introducing Microsoft Silverlight'.

"Here Ravi, take it. I brought this from the library for you." Praveen handed over the book to Ravi. Ravi took the book and apart from feeling the weight of the book, he couldn't think of anything else.

"It is a nice book to refer to for developing Silverlight controls."

"Ok..."

"By Monday you should try to complete this book and after that I think we should be able to complete the work by Friday next week. And by the way I forgot to tell you, I am planning to include Silverlight in our current release itself."

Ravi did not understand whether the correct reaction to the situation was to cry or laugh. 'What the hell? Silverlight in the present release? And reading a four hundred pages book in four days! Hundred pages a day and that too with lots of work pending.'

"Are you serious when you say I should finish this book by Monday?"

"Yes, I am." Noticing the stern expression on Praveen's face, Ravi understood that it was not a joke.

“But...Praveen...I cannot possibly read hundred pages everyday. I cannot even read a novel so fast, and even if I read that fast I cannot guarantee you that I will understand everything in that book.”

“I know that. Even I don’t expect you to complete the entire book. Topics from page number 100 to 180, 250 to 300, 320 to 390 are the most important ones.”

‘80 + 50 + 70 = 200 pages and I don’t even know if I can understand the matter on those pages without going through the first hundred pages.’ This thought made Ravi’s irritation reach new levels. He confronted, “But why do we have to do this Silverlight when Carl had said we can ignore it?”

“The other team which is dealing with the online music stores is using it and got a great review when they presented it to the management team. Also, Ravi you should understand one thing, if we postpone this thing now do you know how long it will take us to include it in our UI?”

“Probably in the next release...”

“And that means 4 more months from now. Isn’t it?”

Ravi understood where the argument was heading now, “Yes...”

“Do you want to wait for four months when we can do it in one week?”

Ashish jumped into the discussion, “Yes, you are correct, Praveen. I think waiting for 4 months is not a correct decision. Yesterday I talked to that team which is using Silverlight and they gave a very good feedback about it and how it improved the usability.”

‘Then you do it...’ these words almost slipped from Ravi’s

mouth but he bit his tongue and controlled his temper.

He thought hard and pulled out a point, "That is okay but how long did they take to complete this stuff?"

"When I asked them the same question, they said four days. Looks like, it is very easy to use," Ashish replied.

"Based on my analysis of the requirements from Carl, looks like we need to touch five different classes and fifteen functions...I don't know if we can replace all that with Silverlight in a week's time. Also it was only during breakfast that you gave me two weeks. Why have we reduced a week from that estimate?"

This question irritated Praveen and he got serious, "Hey Ravi. Listen! There is no negotiation on this aspect. We have decided to do it, as most of the time our customers don't know what they want. We give it to them to make them happy. Given that we are doing it for this release, what you need to do is understand the main contents of the book and execute this thing by Wednesday. Did you get this?"

Ravi thought, 'Poor me...what else can I do in a situation like this?'

"Ok..." it was the only word that escaped from Ravi's mouth and he was so angry with Praveen and Ashish that he avoided eye contact with both of them.

Naina was a mere spectator and she had no part to play in the whole discussion. She kept staring at all three of them and Ravi thought that it would have been good if Naina had come to his rescue. But what can any person, who joined the team just a week ago, do apart from keeping quiet in situations like these?

"Now we have two resources on the UI side. You and Naina. So, it should be relatively easy for us to achieve this one week deadline."

Naina got tensed with his statement and said, "I am still not familiar with all the code."

"In that case Praveen, I can help Ravi with Silverlight," Ashish volunteered.

Praveen was overjoyed with that statement. 'Ashish is such a great resource to have,' he thought.

"This is great news. Take Ashish's help Ravi. Do one thing, you read that book, make a one hour presentation for us on Monday. If I have time I might also help you with this feature."

'Read a four hundred page book in four days and make a presentation on Monday. I have never attempted such a feat before,' thought Ravi.

Praveen was still giving Ravi some advice, "This is challenging work, Ravi. You will get high visibility if you can get this work done in the next one week. Just imagine, man! Everyone who uses your UI will be mesmerised if we provide Silverlight controls. We need to do it."

'Sigh! Visibility! I have heard the word innumerable times in the last three years. Ultimately, my visibility depends on how you project me to our management. Doesn't depend on what I do' thought Ravi and said "Ok...I will try to give a presentation on Monday." But at the same time Ravi found the situation highly confusing. 'Why did Praveen suddenly decide that I should work on Silverlight for this release? Is he trying to take revenge on me? Is this in anyway related to the dinner tonight?' These questions were troubling him.

Meanwhile, Ashish started dictating terms to Ravi, "Try to invite people from other groups also, Ravi. Will be useful for them too."

Not in a mood to argue, Ravi said, "Ok...will send an email

invite to as many people in our group as possible."

'Silverlight, book, presentation, bug fixes...' these thoughts were heating up Ravi's brain. He now understood why most software companies have air conditioning. 'It is for people like me. My fuse would have blown out if not for this chilled environment.'

Then this final discussion with Praveen cleared all his doubts. "Ravi! Looking at your expression I don't think you are still convinced about including Silverlight controls in our current release."

"Yes, I am not..." Ravi eagerly answered his question.

"In that case, why don't you meet with Carl tonight and discuss it with him. I have already written a mail to Carl telling him that everyone is excited about providing Silverlight controls in our current release. But since you are still not convinced about it, I will write another mail to him asking him to meet you tonight. You can discuss it with him and maybe also apprise him of the possible design problems. If he says we need not do it in this release, we can take it off our radar. What say?" smiled Praveen.

Ravi now understood what Praveen was up to. 'Just as I thought, you have decided to keep me busy and take Naina for the date. What a strategy!' Ravi could not think of any answer to his proposal.

"Yes, it is a good idea. Even I will stay back and discuss the issue with Carl," Ashish volunteered.

Ravi wanted to shout, 'You idiot! You are spoiling my love life. You don't understand what is going on between us.' But Rahul's story played in front of him and decided that violence would not get him anything. Being unable to accept that proposal from Praveen, he tried to argue.

He looked at Naina and said, "But Praveen! I had planned

for something else tonight. Is it possible to meet Carl tomorrow morning?"

"No...all of us have seen how late you have come to office today morning. Carl wouldn't be happy if we repeat that again. You meet him tonight and get this issue settled. I am writing to Carl now. Ashish and you meet him tonight and finish this discussion. Ok then..." saying this Praveen turned towards his machine and opened Outlook. It was an indication that the discussion was over and that Ravi could leave.

Ravi came out of the room feeling weak and a bit depressed. He went to the meeting with a feeling that something bad was going to happen. But Praveen had managed to exceed Ravi's expectations. 'Praveen in trying to trap me has assigned me so much work that I am feeling choked now,' thought Ravi and looked at his watch. It showed 12:30 p.m.

❖❖❖

Chapter 10

12:30 p.m.

The Lunch Decision

He got back to his cubicle and picked up a test case to write. He started writing something but the words '...no negotiation...' started ringing in his mind. 'How can Praveen be so rude? This project is as much mine as it is his. Without even asking me for estimates or even trying to know if it is possible for me to execute this feature, he has signed up for it. The worst part is that I cannot complain. Ramnath and Praveen are friends and finally they will make me another Rahul.' As his mind got more and more cluttered with thoughts like these, he searched for a vent for anger building up in him. He got up and walked to the corridor, pulled out his mobile phone, switched it on and dialled his dad.

"Hello."

"Hi dad, Ravi here."

"Hi son! How are you? Is everything going well? I was planning to call you in the evening."

Ravi quickly came to the subject, "Dad, things are going good, except that I am unable to bear my manager's torture."

"Why? What happened?"

Ravi narrated the whole story about how his manager was making him do more and more work. After patiently listening to the entire Ramayana narrated by Ravi, his dad said, "Son, it is your age to work. If that feature gets you good recognition in office then why don't you do it? Don't think of it as a burden. You should enjoy work at this age, my boy. You should learn to work hard."

Ravi called his dad expecting some sympathy from the other end of the line but the statement from his dad irked him more.

"Learn to work hard? What am I doing now? I am already working hard and my manager is pressing me hard to do more."

"You are not the only one, right? You are saying that someone called Ashish is cutting into your work. See him. How does he get time? You should be active like him, only then do you get good recognition anywhere. Also private companies are like this only. Why do you think they pay you more? So that you can sit and do nothing?" questioned his dad.

Fumes were coming out of Ravi's ears. He did not feel like continuing the discussion and said, "Ok dad...will try to adhere to whatever you said. I have some urgent work now."

"Ok then...eat properly and stay healthy."

"Bye."

"Bye."

After hanging his phone, Ravi thought, 'Even my dad doesn't understand my problem and I was expecting my manager to empathise with me. What a joke.' He returned to his desk and started working on the test case but still he could not get his focus right. Finally, after fifteen minutes, he thought he was finished with the test case and did a test run of the case to check if it worked. To his dismay, it failed.

'Damn it! Doesn't work! All because of that meeting! I am unable to focus properly on work. #$@!$@...Praveen is a useless fellow, doesn't know how to treat his reports. Doesn't give an iota of importance to my feelings...is this the way to take revenge? #@$#@' With these thoughts in mind, he tried to debug the test in parallel. Fortunately for him a diversion occurred at that moment. His internal messenger popped up a chat window. The message was from someone called Varun whom he had never met before.

The message read, "Hi Ravi, this is Pradeep here. I am at my friend's desk now. Just wanted to call you for lunch?"

"Now?"

"Yes, why what is the problem?"

"Nothing. Had my breakfast at 10:00, so I was thinking it might be early."

"In that case, let's walk to the Anand mess in Indranagar."

"No...I have work. I cannot come. Also have a meeting at 2:00 p.m. with the test team."

"Hey, we can go and come back in an hour. Don't worry. It is just 12:45 now."

Ravi tried to push Pradeep for a lunch in office, "I think today's menu for the South Indian lunch looked good. Saw it when I was in the cafeteria."

"But you said you wanted some exercise to feel hungry again, right," Pradeep stressed on his point.

This friendly argument was continuing when a mail popped up on Ravi's screen which caught his attention. He opened it and it read...

Subject: Found a cockroach in the South Indian lunch

Message:

I found this cockroach in the South Indian lunch today. Check the picture attached with his mail (captured it with my new iPhone). Found it in the sambar.

Regards,

Sent using iPhone

Immediately his screen buzzed with another message...

Subject: Re: Found a cockroach in the South Indian lunch

Message:

I found one in the North Indian lunch too. Was in the dal. Would advise you people to avoid the lunch at the cafeteria today.

Thanks,

Sent from HTC Touch Diamond

Technology had come to their rescue. Whoever devised the likes of iPhone or Blackberry or WinMobile must have always had business managers in mind when they designed such devices. But most of times they are not used for business purposes but for discussing matters of more vital importance such as these.

This mail settled the issue between Ravi and Pradeep.

"Where are you now?"

"I am on the sixth floor."

"Come to my desk then. Let's go to the Anand Mess."

"Ok...meanwhile, try asking Naresh too."

"Ok..."

Ravi locked his desktop and went to Naresh's cubicle and told him about the plan to go to Indranagar for lunch. Naresh agreed but said, "One minute, Ravi. There are more replies to that cockroach mail. People are analysing where those cockroaches could have come from." As he said this, he started laughing.

"Where show me?" Ravi looked at the monitor.

Reply...

Subject: Re: Found a cockroach in the South Indian lunch

Message:

We should blacklist this vendor and throw him out. That picture of the sambar with a cockroach in it was disgusting.

The series continued...

'I see that the coackroach is alive in the picture. In such a case is it because of the unclean premises?' read one mail.

'Even if it is because of the unclean premises, it is the responsibility of the vendor to maintain cleanliness. That space belongs to the vendor, right?' read another.

Someone from the cafeteria committee, which was a group of employees representing SOS employees for the vendor, got into the discussion.

'Maintaining cleanliness is the duty of SOS. Vendor is not responsible for that...'

People turned their ire towards the cafeteria committee.

'This is the second time this month. And the cafeteria committee doesn't do anything except for sending mails to the SOS-Hyderabad group? That cockroach in the sambar might be alive but the one in the dal is dead. It is clearly a fault on the vendor's side. What action are you going to take against him?'

The email fight worsened when another person from the cafeteria committee joined the fight.

'We have reported the matter to the facilities people who actually deal with the vendor...they said they will take the necessary action...'

An irritated person replied...

'What is your responsibility then? Why do you send mails to us?'

Reply...

'We escalate your problems to the facilities.'

Reply...

'I know how to write a mail. I don't need you between myself and the facilities...'

Though Ravi wasn't amused with such mails, Naresh was almost rolling on the floor with laughter. He somehow treated that SOS-Hyderabad discussion forum as an entertainment channel. The mail over-reprimanding the vendor had turned into a fight between employees.

From prior experience both Ravi and Naresh knew that the thread was not going to solve their problems. Ravi said, "This problem can never be solved dude. Have seen it happen many times in the last few years."

"True. It is better to eat at Anand daily. It is better than our vendor," said Naresh.

"Hello..." someone greeted them from behind. Ravi and Naresh turned around and saw Pradeep standing near the cubicle.

"Shall we go?" asked Pradeep.

"Yeah sure. First let's go to the washroom and then go to Indranagar," said Ravi.

"Sure and by the way he is my friend Varun." After greeting each other, the gang of four walked toward the lifts. Ravi came to know from the introduction that Varun joined SOS five months ago and that he had recently moved from Bangalore to Hyderabad.

❖❖❖

Chapter 11

The Walk to Anand

01:00 p.m.

They started walking towards the main gate when Ravi started the conversation.

"Dude...do you know what kind of trouble you got me into this morning?"

"Even I wanted to ask you about the same thing. Why were you making all those faces in the cafeteria?"

"Man! The person standing behind me was my manager."

"What!! He was your manager. Oh! Now I understand why he was standing there and staring at us," Pradeep started roaring with laughter. "Dude...your manager would have got the shock of his life. He had such a pathetic look on his face," saying this he continued laughing.

Naresh and Varun grew curious about the incident and Naresh enquired, "What happened?"

Ravi did not look as amused as Pradeep was with the incident. "In the morning I came to the cafeteria along with my manager and I met Pradeep there. The first thing he asked me was 'Is your manager still torturing you...' Dude! My manager stared at both of us and went away. I don't know what kind of revenge he will take on me?" saying this, a wilted look came over his face.

Listening to this, Varun and Naresh started laughing too.

"Dudes...I am feeling scared about the situation and you are laughing at me?"

“Chill dude! Think positively. Under normal circumstances, you would never have got an opportunity to tell your manager that he is an idiot. Now that information got conveyed to him. Be happy about something. Think positively!” said Pradeep and he continued laughing.

Noticing that people were laughing at him, Ravi decided to change the topic and said, “Shall we take an auto to Indranagar?”

“Auto? You said you had a heavy breakfast. Let’s walk. Good for our health.”

“What? In this sun?”

“Hey...don’t behave like a girl. Fifteen minutes of exposure to the sun will not make you dark,” argued Pradeep.

“It is not about getting dark. It is hot.”

“Don’t worry, Ravi I will buy you that ‘fair and handsome’ cream, you should be glowing in a week,” Varun tried pulling Ravi’s leg.

Ravi felt uncomfortable as everyone was cracking jokes on him and he continued, “Dudes! I have a meeting to attend in the afternoon. I will be late by the time we go and comeback.”

“Hey...tell me a day which goes by without meetings. Also don’t talk about work once we have crossed our office premises. It irritates me,” said Naresh. Pradeep and Varun nodded in agreement.

‘Ha! At least this gang shares the same feelings as I do,’ thought Ravi.

Since three of them wanted to walk to the mess, Ravi had no other option but to agree to it. They had to cross the road before they could continue their walk and were waiting for the traffic to clear. Lots of autos were parked in front of their office. The autos were waiting for customers who regularly travel from SOS to Indranagar or to the interiors of Hyderabad.

"Auto sir?" asked an auto-driver who was waiting for passengers.

"No..." said Pradeep.

"Ouch!! You idiot! Can't you see," Naresh started shouting at an auto. That auto had managed to get its tyre over Naresh's right foot. Fortunately, the auto was empty and Naresh escaped unhurt.

But Naresh was badly irritated and he went to the auto and started screaming at the driver.

" #@$%#@... Can't you see the road and drive?"

The auto driver was eager to continue the fight and said, "Control your tongue. What happened? Why are you shouting at me?"

"You drove over my foot, you idiot."

"You don't know where to walk on the road. It is not my mistake. Who asked you to come in the path of my auto?"

Naresh did not relent and said, "I was walking properly. You are driving with eyes at the back of your head. By the way who asked you to park here? Do you think this is some auto stand?"

"I will park wherever I want to. Who are you to ask me? Is this your property?"

Naresh's irritation reached new levels. The *auto-wallah* was scolding Naresh in front of his office. Naresh believed that it was on his home turf that the *auto-wallah* was plying. So blinded with this sense of security, he continued the fight.

Pointing his finger towards SOS, Naresh said, “I am an employee of this company. It is in front of my office that you have parked, so I have all the rights to ask what you are doing here.”

“Huh! You are just an employee here. I am a local. I will park wherever I want to.”

The argument was picking up heat and more auto drivers started coming to the aid of their friend. Having heard the word ‘LOCAL’ and noticing that more auto drivers were gathering at that place, Pradeep sensed trouble. He entered the scene and pulled Naresh aside and tried to calm him down.

“Calm down. What is the use of arguing with him? We are getting late.”

Naresh did not listen and shouted, “I will get your licence cancelled. My uncle is police commissioner.”

The *auto-wallah* was defiant. He had obviously heard the same sentence from many people. So he shouted back, “So what? Go and complain. He is my uncle too.”

Varun and Ravi also joined Pradeep and managed to pull Naresh out of that area and make him walk towards Indranagar.

“If not for you, I would have planted two punches on his face. Would have broken his nose,” Naresh was still agitated.

“Naresh is a hero. Had an auto going over his foot and is now talking about punching the driver,” Varun joked and started laughing.

Ravi responded to Naresh’s statement, “You and punching that fellow? Did you ever look at yourself in the mirror?”

“Why, what is wrong with me?” said Naresh.

“You talk as if you are Salman Khan. With your bony physique, you will not get up for a week if he punches you. Keep your cool when you are on the roads, dude."

Pradeep winked at Ravi and tried scaring Naresh, "Yeah, what if that fellow pulls out a knife, Naresh?"

The answer was instant. "You people are there," said Naresh trying to count on his friends.

The others seized the opportunity. "Oh! You thought we would come to your rescue? We will run away if he pulls out a knife," said Ravi.

"Yes, but we are also true friends, dude. We will call the police if he stabs you," said Pradeep.

"Yes, we will fight your case in the courts and make him get the punishment for whatever he might have done to you," Varun joined the party.

"What! You will let him stab me and then fight my case in the court? Is it?" Naresh was coming to his senses. 'These people are capable of doing something like this,' he thought.

Ravi tried scaring Naresh a bit more, "Say even if we rescued you today. What about tomorrow? That driver is a regular face at the auto stand and he was saying that he was a local fellow."

"Oh! You mean that fellow can attack me tomorrow?" said Naresh, who the others noticed was getting anxious with every statement of theirs.

"Yeah, it is possible. The other day I read in the newspapers about an incident where an *auto-wallah* attacked someone two days after a quarrel with the person," said Pradeep, adding a realistic touch to the episode.

"That is why you should control your tongue when you are on the road. You are no karate fighter," added Ravi.

Naresh was trembling with fear. But the last statement from Ravi gave him a new idea. 'These days I am free in the evenings, I will learn karate,' thought Naresh.

"Karate! Yeah, I forgot dudes. Since a long time I wanted to learn karate. Do you know any karate institute nearby," enquired Naresh.

"What! You want to learn karate to fight with auto drivers," commented Pradeep and started laughing. Ravi and Varun joined the laughter.

Naresh turned silent and started following them to Anand. He was deeply thinking about how he should fight with that auto driver if he attacks him tomorrow.

"By the way, is the police commissioner really your uncle?" enquired Ravi.

"I don't even know the name of our police commissioner. I just wanted to frighten him," said Naresh.

"What an idea, *sirjee*!" commented Varun and continued, "but that fellow did not seem perturbed even after you made that statement."

"Yeah...that is what I thought too," said Naresh and he fell quiet again. 'Does that mean that the driver is a real *goonda*. He doesn't even seem to care for the police,' he thought and the thought frightened him more.

When have you come to Hyderabad and become acquainted with its surroundings, the first person you think about when in trouble is Lord Balaji. The last time that Naresh visited the Chilkur Balaji temple, he got the US Visa issued without any hassles. His devotion for the Lord intensified after that visit. Now in fear, he started praying to the Lord again. 'Lord, if you save me from that driver, I will come to Chilkur and walk 108 times around your temple.' The thought that he had put his wish at the Lord's feet gave him some confidence. 'Balaji will save me. I have that confidence,' he thought and turned a bit more cheerful again.

By the time they reached Anand, it was almost 1:10 p.m. Pradeep ordered for four full meals and then sat at a table. The ambience at Anand was much different from that at SOS. Wooden chairs, greasy tables, cement floor and flies everywhere. It was opposite the plush Subway and Domino's pizza stores which seemed to mock at Anand.

Though their gang occasionally visited both Subway and Anand, they somehow preferred the 'Indian' lunch at Anand compared to the westernised food served at those places. And the argument came up again.

"Hey, why not go to Subway? Healthy food?" asked Pradeep

"No...I don't want to go to Subway. Bread and raw vegetables, yuck..." Naresh replied.

"What is so healthy about it, dude? I put cheese into it and it is as good as the food we eat here," said Varun.

"Yeah, costly option too. I don't know the name of half the sauces there and also, I feel embarrassed whenever I go there," said Ravi.

"Embarrassed? Why?" enquired Pradeep.

"Once, I went in and asked him to put cabbage in it and there was a kid standing beside me who corrected me saying that it is lettuce and not cabbage. To this day, I don't know what is the difference between both the items," revealed Ravi. Hearing him others started laughing.

"Ok...let's drop that idea then."

"So, how is your project going on, Pradeep," asked Ravi.

“My project got scrapped two weeks ago. Right now, I am on the bench.”

“Bench? That is a risky thing? Isn’t it?”

“Yeah, kind of. I was given a month’s time to find a new opportunity within the company. Scouting for work now.”

“Ok,” said Ravi.

“Are there any openings in your groups?” enquired Pradeep.

“Not any I can think of,” said Ravi.

“Same here,” added Varun.

“No problem, I have an interview scheduled with another group tomorrow. I think I should be doing well. They told me that the interview would be in Java. I am good at it. Just wanted to know if there are any more open positions.”

Meanwhile, the food was served and they started their lunch. Naresh called out to the waiter and asked him for four rotis.

Varun enquired with Pradeep, “But Pradeep, last week you said you would be attending some internal interview this Monday. What happened to that?”

“Oh that! Don’t remind me about that, dude. It was a bad experience.”

“Why? What happened?” asked Ravi.

“Did you fail to answer any of the questions?” asked Naresh.

“No...I gave the interview well. In the last round, they also told me that I am a good candidate and that I would be selected to that position.”

“So, what happened after that?” asked Naresh.

“That afternoon when I was having lunch in the cafeteria, one of my old project-mate met me. He asked me how things were going on and in the course of our discussion I told him about my interview in the morning. In the evening, I was shocked to know that he was given that position and I was denied it."

"What? How is that possible, dude?"

"Apparently, the person to whom I gave the information was also on the bench. He shared a very good relation with the project manager of that team. This dude went and confronted that manager as to how he, who was such a great friend of his, did not consider him for that position. That manager somehow ran the show behind the scenes and got my name removed from the list and this person was offered the job."

"How did you get this information, dude?" enquired Ravi.

"This same person who replaced me met me in the evening and started boasting about the achievement."

"And you did nothing?" asked Naresh.

"What can I do, dude?"

Naresh grew furious and said, "That is ridiculous. You should have slapped him."

"This is corporate world, not some labour *adda*. Also this is recession time, dude. That fellow himself was saying that he was very close to the project manager. I will get fired if I confront him and do something stupid. Better to try for other opportunities."

"Naresh is in a slapping mood today. Thought of slapping the auto driver there and now is talking about slapping colleagues," joked Ravi.

Naresh ignored that and said, "I don't think what you did was correct. At least you should have complained to the HR team."

"HR team?" repeated Varun giving a sarcastic laugh.

“They are there for purposes like this, right?” asked Naresh.

“I personally think that approaching HR is not a great idea.”

“How can you say like that?” demanded Naresh.

“See dude, you are less valuable to this company compared to your manager. Replacing you is easier than replacing your manager. So if you unnecessarily create a scene in front of them, it becomes easy for that manager to convince them to push you out of the company.”

“How is that possible? He is telling the truth, right!”

“This is no harassment case between Pradeep and that manager. It is just a matter of politics. What will he tell the HR team? That he was replaced by someone else? What is the proof? What if the manager managed to show the other guy as a genuinely interviewed person? Do you have any proof for this?”

“No...” Naresh was seeing the reality. “Yeah, you are correct. There is no way he can prove his case.”

“Yes and that is why I was quiet and started searching for other opportunities. It is not worth fighting with the management, dude,” said Pradeep.

“This office politics, it is disgusting. Managers are such idiots. They are here just to screw our lives,” ranted Naresh.

Pradeep was one who never blamed others for his misery. So he said, “Managers are also human beings, Naresh. What would you do in a situation where your friend comes to you and asks you for a position in your group? You would have done the same thing which that manager did...is it not?”

“Yeah maybe, but this is too much. I don’t know how you are able to digest this fact and still empathise with that idiot. I don’t like these managers. My manager is a sadist. He makes me and

Ravi work hard and doesn't give us proper appraisals. Especially if you take the case of Ravi, he knows more technologies than most of us in the team and still he does not receive the amount of recognition he should receive."

Ravi felt elated at the fact that his friend was praising him. 'Naresh is my best friend,' he thought.

Suddenly Varun had a doubt, "What does it take to be a manager? What should I do to become a manager? Wherefrom they get people like those?"

"Good question," said Ravi. "I don't know what it exactly takes to be a manager. But I think maybe, we should mentor a group of people, show some great design skills and demonstrate risk taking potential."

While Ravi was blabbering something, Naresh called the waiter and reminded him about the rotis and then jumped into the discussion again.

"If you ask me, yours is an ideal answer. I personally think nothing like that is required to become a manager," said Naresh.

Ravi was surprised and asked him, "Then what else is required?"

"The most important requirement is that you should be able to screw the lives of your reports. The second is that in the process of screwing other's lives your life shouldn't get affected."

Ravi got interested and enquired, "Any examples? I did not understand what do you meant by that."

Naresh started explaining, "In my previous project, my manager once called me and asked me to add a column to a table on a particular webpage."

"Ok..."

"I went to my place and checked the website and did not find the particular page that my manager had told me about. I thought maybe, I was looking at the wrong code base and went back and told him about that," saying this Naresh stopped to drink a glass of water.

Ravi was the one who always wanted to hear a story without any discontinuity in narration, so he prodded Naresh. "So what did he say?" he asked.

Naresh felt happy that his story had aroused some interest in others. He gulped water and said, "Don't get too excited, dude. I will tell you."

He continued, "My manager thought for a minute and told me that my observation was correct and the page did not exist. So it seems that his requirement was that I should design the page first and then add a table and then add this particular column to it."

"Ok...so you had to deduce all that from a single statement?" said Ravi.

"Wait! The story doesn't end here. Then I asked him where the data that I should add to that column will come from. To that he told me that it will come from the data warehouse. When he told me that the value will come from the warehouse, I told him that we don't have a warehouse and he told me that it was a part of the requirement, that is, to build one."

"Build a complete warehouse!" gasped Ravi. "But that is too much of work, right!"

"It still does not end here, dude. I went back to my place and for a day I did an analysis on how to build this warehouse on top of our existing database. At the end of the day I noticed that the data for that new column, which that manager mentioned about in the requirements, wasn't getting tracked in our database itself."

Ravi was surprised and at the same time felt happy that he had company. 'It isn't just me who was getting tortured here,' he thought.

Meanwhile, Naresh continued, "You know what my manager said when I told him about that?"

"What did he say?"

"He said, I was supposed to understand all that from the one line he told me. He scolded me for repeatedly coming to him for clarifications. He told me that if I have to grow and become a manager like him, then I should be able to analyse his one-liners without repeatedly coming to him for help. So from that one line requirement which looked so simple in the beginning, I ended up building a new webpage, a data warehouse, changed our database structure, wrote data transformation scripts between warehouse and database and finally modified our business code to track the value that he initially asked for."

"Wow! That is too much, right?! You never told us anything about this," said Pradeep.

"Never got the chance, dude."

"But it is crazy. So many changes to code in one release?" said Ravi.

"Do you think I didn't protest? I gave him many reasons as to why we shouldn't do this big a change. But apparently, the project manager in the billing group had got his team to implement a data warehouse and this dude here did not want to be seen as the one who couldn't do something similar."

"So, for him to look competitive he makes us work like donkeys, is it?"

"Wait! You haven't heard another joke yet."

"What is that?" asked Ravi.

"The estimate. He gave me seven days to do all these changes."

"What?!"

"Yes...you heard it right. The billing team had done it in fifteen days for their project, it seems. So, this dude gave me half the time that they took to complete it. If you are surprised listening to this story from me, you should have seen my face when my manager told me about the estimate. After bargaining with him for a very long time, he agreed to give me fifteen days to complete it."

"Is it some competition or what? We are supposed to be competing with our competitors outside SOS, not with our own teams within SOS, right!" said Ravi.

"I think for that manager the other team's manager was his competitor when it came to promotions," said Pradeep and laughed.

"Yeah, I think so. After meeting with my manager, I went to that billing team and asked them as to what exactly they did for their product and I was shocked to learn that in fifteen days they actually executed half the stuff I was assigned to do. Dudes! You know what? It ultimately took me six weeks to build the whole thing that he asked me to complete in seven days."

"Your manager sucks, man!" said Varun.

"Yeah right, he sucks. Even after successfully completing this big a feature, he scolded me numerous times for not sticking to the original estimates. Anyway, you haven't heard what happened in the end," said Naresh.

"What? There is more?" Ravi asked in a surprised tone.

"Yes, on the day of the release we got a mail from our manager saying that he got another opportunity in some other team and was leaving. And that was followed by congratulatory mails from everyone saying that he got some complex portions of the project executed such as the warehouse. I slogged and he got the recognition."

Pradeep, Ravi and Varun seemed to agree with Naresh on that point and nodded in agreement.

Naresh continued, "You know why I shifted to this project? That manager forced me to do so many changes in six weeks that the project went into an unstable state. I started getting support calls in the middle of the night, almost on a daily basis. So, finally after two months I couldn't bear it anymore and shifted here. Now, do you understand what it takes to be a manager? He took all the credit and I became a donkey in the end."

Suddenly Pradeep felt that he also had something to add to the discussion, "I forgot. There is one more important quality that is required to become a manager."

"What is it?"

"You should learn five buzzwords in each technology. Say for example, when it comes to database systems you should know names like SSAS, SSRS, SSIS, ETL and maybe SQL broker."

"What are they?" enquired Ravi.

"Who knows? But you should know a buzzword and then a brief description of it."

"Ok...and then?"

"When you are in meetings and someone comes up with a problem, you should fire this buzzword and then extrapolate how it can be useful."

"How is that necessary for becoming a manager?"

"Dude...do you know what SSIS is?"

"No."

"Most probably 9 out of 10 people in a meeting would never know what it is or what it exactly does, and that is what you should take advantage of. Show them that you know something that they don't know, and people will keep thinking that you are a Bond. And that is what finally gives you recognition."

"Ok..." Ravi was getting more and more confused. He had never analysed things from that point of view.

Naresh joined the discussion again and said, "True...true...also there is one last quality that is required the most. You should learn words like 'awesome', 'great', 'superb', 'amazing' and keep using them as frequently as you can, especially when you are talking to the client. A bit of American or UK slang/accent is also great."

Amused at this kind of an analysis, Pradeep and Varun started laughing.

"Ok...but still it is somewhat difficult for me to believe that things like these are more important than hard work," said Ravi.

"Believe what you want to. I believe in what I say," concluded Naresh.

❖❖❖

Chapter 12

A Plan is Hatched

01:20 p.m.

Ravi was enjoying the conversation till that moment. After the intense discussion, everyone started concentrating on finishing the food in their plates. At the same time, Naresh called the waiter and reminded him about the rotis again.

"Hey, how many times should I tell you? Get them quickly," he shouted.

"Yes sir. Two minutes, sir," the waiter said politely and rushed to the kitchen. But before he could go and remind someone in the kitchen about the rotis, someone called him to get water. The waiter hurriedly ran towards the voice to attend to the table and coolly forgot about the order again.

Meanwhile, Ravi who was now eating silently was thinking hard about the problem he had at hand. He suddenly remembered that he wanted to take Naina out on a date but was requested by his manager to stay back for the night. The expression on his face immediately changed showing that he was in deep thought. Noticing the change, Pradeep enquired, "What happened, Ravi? Why this sudden change in your mood?"

"Nothing. Leave it. I was just thinking about the project," Ravi tried to keep the issue a secret. But his friends were not ones who would leave him so easily.

"Tell us. What is the issue? If not with us who else will you share your problems with," said Naresh.

Ravi was desperately waiting to share his story with anyone.

Having got no consolation from his dad, he felt that at least his friends would understand his problem. He decided to share his story with them.

"Ok, I will tell you but promise me that you will not share it with others."

"We promise you," said Pradeep. Naresh and Varun nodded in agreement.

Ravi narrated them the whole story on how he fell for Naina, his plans for a dinner with her tonight, Praveen's interest in Naina and how Praveen had thwarted his plans for the dinner. Having intently listened to the full story, Naresh was the first one to react.

"You have already faced two failures in matters like this before. Why are you trying to become a donkey again?"

"What! Ravi has some love failure history, is it?" enquired Pradeep.

"Yeah! You don't know the stories?" asked Naresh.

"No...come on. I want to listen to this flashback first."

Ravi was getting embarrassed and he protested, "Why is that required now?"

Naresh decided to make fun of Ravi and said, "I will tell them this story first and then we can get back to the present problem."

Ravi got agitated and shouted, "Dude! You think I don't know about you?"

This aggression made Naresh become defensive. "What did I do? I never had any love history."

"I know. I have seen you staring at Deepa's photographs on your computer screen," Ravi leaked Naresh's story.

"Who is Deepa?" enquired Varun.

"She is a tester who works in that banking project. Her team is located on the 3rd floor," Ravi was going on and on.

Naresh was getting embarrassed. He never thought that someone knew so much about his private life.

"What Naresh! You and Deepa are in love?" questioned Pradeep.

"Only a one-sided love," Ravi explained. "Three months ago both our teams went for an outing together. That was where I noticed Naresh always trying to find a place beside her. That is, when we gathered for group photographs or for playing games, he was always trying to find a place beside her. Two weeks after that I went to his cubicle and he was fully engrossed with something on his monitor."

"Enough!" shouted Naresh. "Stop it, Ravi...you have already spoken enough stuff here."

"No...I will finish my statement," said Ravi. Pradeep giggled and said, "Yeah...continue. We want to listen to this story too."

"Where was I? Yeah right! When I saw him staring at his monitor so much, I decided to take a look and peeped at his monitor. Naresh was looking at one particular photograph from the team outing, where Deepa and he were standing beside each other. Our dude was so lost that he did not notice me."

Naresh was embarrassed and deeply hurt with Ravi spreading his story like this. "Ravi! You shared my story with them, right. Now even if you plead with me I am not going to stop narrating your stories."

Ravi realised that he had made a big mistake. In his enthusiasm to stop Naresh from narrating his history, Ravi had brought him to a point where there was no stopping Naresh.

Varun and Pradeep were enjoying the conversation. "Yeah, you are correct. Ravi, now that you have talked so much about Naresh, you shouldn't interrupt him now," said Pradeep.

Unable to do anything else, Ravi kept quiet.

"Ok guys! Let me start. Both of us joined SOS in the same year. In our first year here, there was a girl by name Neha. Our dude was friend with her for almost a year. In that one year, whenever Neha worked late our dude worked late and whenever she came early he used to come early. He used to take extra burden and complete her work. I told him so many times to go and propose her, but this idiot never had the courage to do so and postponed it for a very long time."

"Then what happened?" asked Pradeep.

"Then what! One day, she walked to him and told him that she had some good news to share. And when our dude asked what? She said a new developer who joined SOS just two weeks back fell in love with her and that even she started liking him."

"Wow! So it is not the first time that he is facing some competition from someone in his group. What happened when she told him that way? Did Ravi turn into a 'Devdas'?" asked Varun.

"Initially, it was a shock for him. Whenever the issue cropped up in our discussions, he used to cry but gradually he came out of it. I think it took him around six months to come out of that shock. The next incident is the funniest one. Last year, one of our client representatives called Laura visited us. She was a beautiful woman who looked to be in her early twenties. Our dude here fell in love with her."

"What? Love across boundaries? Ravi! You are too much, dude! What happened after that?" Pradeep showed deep interest in the matter.

Ravi was getting embarrassed and he tried to stop this show. “Hey Naresh! Stop it...please dude. Give me some solution to the present problem. This is all past.”

“No, I won’t stop. Why did you bring Deepa into discussion here? I will complete this story too,” Naresh was defiant.

“Yeah...yeah...we want to know this story too,” demanded Varun.

“I will tell you the story. Don’t worry,” Naresh continued. “Ravi was so much influenced by her that he was always ready to do any feature that she requested the team to do. He regularly volunteered to do all the phone discussions with her and was almost constantly in touch with her for around four months. Even here I suggested him to propose her if he liked her so much. But again, our dude lacked courage. However, there was one thing that he did which surprised me.”

“What was that?” enquired Pradeep.

“One day, all of us got a mail from Laura thanking Ravi for the nice birthday gift that he had sent to her. Apparently, Ravi called up some gift shop in US and asked them to deliver flowers and a birthday cake to her. But you know what? That mail was a shocker to Ravi,” Naresh continued the suspense.

“Why? He should have been happy?” asked Varun. Ravi’s face was turning red with embarrassment.

“Yeah, under normal circumstances he should have been happy. But what happened here was different. The mail said, ‘My kids Charlie and Harry liked that cake very much’,” telling this Naresh started laughing.

Ravi now entered the discussion. “What can I do, dude? She was not wearing a ring when she visited us last year and I thought that she was unmarried. Never thought, she was a divorcee.”

"Hey! What if she was divorced, dude? You should have continued that relation," joked Pradeep and started laughing.

"Yeah...you should have continued that relation. It was like a 'buy 1 get 2 free' offer, dude! Marry her and get 2 kids free," said Naresh and continued laughing.

"So what happened after that mail?" asked Pradeep.

"What happened? Ravi gradually reduced his calls with her and three months after that mail Laura moved to some other company."

"Oh! So sad...do you miss her, Ravi?" Pradeep tried pulling Ravi's leg.

"Enough dudes. Now that you know the story, why don't you help me with the current situation," said Ravi.

Varun who was quiet till now joined the discussion. "I don't like all these love stories. You all become dogs, Vodafone-dogs, at the end of the day. Be like me, man."

"Be like you? What are you suggesting?" asked Ravi.

"I have had around six affairs till today. There is no mental attachment involved and you don't feel deceived at the end of it. You would have had your share of fun. This is life, dude!" said Varun.

Ravi was taken aback by that statement. He had never seen anyone with such a frivolous attitude towards love and girls. He tried to say something, "But..." but he couldn't find any words.

Varun continued, "No ifs and buts, dude. I have had long-term relationships with two girls and four were just one night stands with girls I encountered at various places. My suggestion is that you too try something like that with this girl whom you are talking about. Take her to a pub, get her drunk and do the necessary."

Pradeep had nothing to say in a matter like this but Naresh was a person with conservative views. He demanded, "Hey! It is stupidity. You might get AIDS and on top of it you are playing with the lives of so many girls. Didn't anyone of them ask you to marry then?"

Varun was hurt with that argument and said, "I am not playing with the lives of anyone here. The girls wilfully got along with me. Yeah...two of them did plead me to marry them but I did not agree. Who knows? Who else those ******* slept with?"

Naresh continued the argument, "Hey! How can you call your former girlfriends like that? You share the same character as they do? What happened to those girls then? How did they leave you?"

"Don't comment on my character, okay. I am just enjoying my life. You thought those girls would eternally wait for me? They got married to guys like you," Varun gave a sarcastic laugh.

That last statement irked Naresh and he got up from his seat with a scornful look on his face. Given a chance, he wanted to punch Varun in his stomach.

Pradeep sensed that the argument was going out of control, so he chipped in. He managed to make Naresh sit in his chair and said, "Calm down fellows. We are not here to fight amongst ourselves. No more talk on this subject."

Ravi joined, "Yes, I am not looking for a suggestion like what you have given me just now. I am really in love with her, so give me some other suggestion." He changed the topic.

But this discussion did break the relations between Naresh and Varun. 'This fellow Varun thinks he is smart. Let me get back to the office and I will kick Pradeep's ass. Idiot! Doesn't know whom to have friendship with,' thought Naresh. Varun was thinking similar stuff about Naresh. Naresh was an ill-tempered person and now his temper was on a high.

Anand is a small place but is always bustling with people, as many software employees come here for lunch. Owing to the heavy rush, the waiter forgot Naresh's order again and again. It was nearly 1:35 and still the rotis were not served.

Naresh tried to vent his fury at the waiters at Anand. "Useless fellows, I asked them for rotis about fifteen minutes back and they haven't served them yet. Let me talk to their owner," saying this he got up.

"Hey! We are almost full, why this fight for rotis again. Call the waiter and tell him that we don't need the rotis," said Pradeep.

"No! This fellow needs to learn how to behave with customers." He walked towards the place where the owner of Anand was seated.

Varun was happy that Naresh left the table. Meanwhile, Ravi asked the team again. "Guys, any suggestions? How do I come out of this situation?"

"You want to go out with the girl tonight and you don't want your manager to come in the way, right?" asked Pradeep.

"Yes."

"Then what I can think of is, since the girl is also working on UI, you tell your manager that she has to attend the meeting," said Varun.

"But I don't think he will agree to it."

Pradeep had a brainwave. "I think I have got a perfect idea for this. I have seen people dealing with similar scenarios in movies. I would suggest the same thing here. When we go out now, buy two laxative tablets from the medical shop. Mix it in your manager's coffee and he will be away on leave for the rest of the day. He will not even have the energy to drive back home," giggled Pradeep and continued, "then you ask Naina to stay back for the meeting in the night and instead of going to some restaurant, you can bring her to either Domino's or Subway here tonight."

Ravi liked the idea of making Naina stay back for the night but was somewhat scared at the prospect of mixing a laxative in Praveen's coffee. "I don't think I can mix that thing in his coffee. What if he knows I mixed something?"

"You behave like a child, Ravi. How will your manager know that you have mixed something in this coffee? If you think that the coffee with these tablets will have a different taste, try adding more espresso to the drink."

"Yes, I like this idea," said Varun.

However hard Ravi thought he could find no other great plan and finally he too started liking this idea and agreed to it. "Ok then, I will buy a couple of tablets and add them to his coffee."

Pradeep exuded confidence in his plan. "This plan cannot fail, Ravi. He will not trouble you today."

Meanwhile, the gang heard some commotion near the entrance of the hotel. They all turned that way and saw that Naresh had picked up a fight with the waiter and the owner.

"Guys! Naresh has ended up creating a mess. Let's wrap up the lunch now," said Pradeep.

All of them got up, washed their hands and then caught hold of Naresh. Pradeep asked Ravi to take Naresh out of the hotel.

"Sorry sir! My friend is in a bad mood today," Pradeep apologised to the hotel owner to which the owner replied, "tell your friend to be in his senses. Today you are here to save him;

otherwise we were planning to throw him out."

Pradeep apologised again and paid the bill. He came out and saw that Naresh was still in an agitated mood. "Hey! It is okay. Don't get so agitated over silly issues, dude. You will unnecessarily spoil your own health," said Pradeep.

"Yeah, right!" added Ravi while Varun kept quiet.

Pradeep tried to change the topic and said, "Ravi, you said you wanted to buy some tablets, right. We will be walking towards SOS, you buy those tablets and join us."

Not in a mood to walk with Varun, Naresh said, "I will come with you, Ravi." Meanwhile, Varun said, "I have an urgent work to attend to. Why don't both of us take an auto?"

Ravi agreed to this and both Ravi and Naresh went to buy the tablets and Pradeep and Varun boarded a shared auto to SOS.

"That Varun is a stupid. Doesn't know how to behave with others..." Naresh was fuming with anger.

Ravi tried to calm him down. "Forget it, dude. Don't get agitated over everything."

Meanwhile Naresh himself tried to change the topic and said, "What are these tablets for?"

Ravi explained Pradeep's plan in detail. "Wow! Good plan," said Naresh. "Great idea! These days Praveen is just torturing me with lots of work. This should serve him good."

"Hope it goes well," said Ravi and both of them bought the tablets and then started their journey back to office.

❖❖❖

Chapter 13

A Costly Mistake

02:10 p.m.

By the time Ravi and Naresh reached their cubicles, they were late for the test team's meeting.

"Should we go to this meeting now or skip it?" Ravi asked Naresh.

"Let's skip it. Otherwise Praveen will strip us naked in front of everyone. Last time I was late to a meeting by five minutes, he said, 'You have wasted 30 minutes of our time'."

"How did he calculate that?"

"Six people waiting for me makes it 6 x 5=thirty minutes, it seems. I am not going to the meeting now. He will say something or the other," saying this Naresh walked towards his desk.

Ravi too decided against going to the meeting and sat at his desk. The first thing he did was to open his mailbox. The first mail he noticed was some mail indicating that a critical component failed in the production environment. As usual, Ashish replied to that mail stating that he was working on the issue. Apart from that issue nothing much had happened.

Ravi then opened his environment and started working on his test cases. Though he was working on the tests, his mind was preoccupied with thoughts on how to win the game today. 'How do I get a coffee laced with this laxative? How do I make him drink it?' These thoughts were troubling him. He worked that way for about an hour when his mobile rang.

He looked at the number and it was from Ganesh, Ravi's second roommate.

"Hello," said Ravi.

"#@#^%$#...*******... #@$$@#..." Ganesh was furious about something and did not even show the courtesy to reply with a 'Hello'. He was shouting so loudly that a phone might not have been required between Ravi and Ganesh.

"Dude...calm down," shouted Ravi.

But the shouts did not subside. "$#@@#@... ^##^@...*****" they continued.

"Hey! Calm down...otherwise I will switch off my phone."

This statement had the desirable effect on Ganesh and he calmed down, "You idiot! You almost got me beaten up today." He was still shouting.

It was the first sensible statement that Ganesh had uttered. Though Ravi could understand the sentence, he was unable to understand what Ganesh meant.

"I almost got you beaten up? What did I do?" demanded Ravi.

"Ass...why did you lock the door when I was still inside the apartment?" shouted Ganesh.

That statement made Ravi instantly realise his mistake. 'How stupid of me!' and he said "Oh! I...I...was in a hurry and forgot about you, Ganesh. Sorry for that. How did you come out?"

The sorry from Ravi calmed down Ganesh a bit but not fully. He was still fuming with rage. "How can you forget? We have been residing here for almost two years now and you still forget who lives in the apartment with you?"

"Sorry dude...I am extremely sorry for that. I had a meeting at eight and I was in a hurry. Where are you now? In the apartment or in office?"

"I am in office now. Because of you I faced so many troubles today that I am gonna murder you if I see you tonight."

"What troubles did you face? You could have called someone and they would have opened that lock for you," asked Ravi.

"You think I cannot think properly. I called you up twice between eight and nine in the morning and you rejected both the calls. After that you switched off your mobile phone."

Ravi now remembered the two calls to his mobile in the morning. "So you were the one who called me? Sorry dude...I was late to that meeting and my manager was shouting at me, so I switched off my phone. You should have called Vijay. He took my bike. He could have come back."

"I called him up and that idiot forgot his mobile phone at home. I don't know his office number."

"What I actually meant when I said 'called someone' was that you could have shouted for help. The security guard or our neighbours would have helped you."

Ganesh was a bit exhausted with all that shouting and his voice was back to normal again. He tried to share his pathetic story with his roommate so that he could find some solace. "I did what you just said and that was what landed me in trouble."

"Trouble? What happened?"

Just at this moment, Praveen came to Ravi's cubicle and he stood there seeing that Ravi was busy on the phone. Ravi saw him and gestured that he will come to his room in ten minutes. Having conveyed the message that he wanted to talk to Ravi, Praveen left the place.

Meanwhile, Ganesh continued to narrate his story. "As both of you were unavailable, I tried calling for help. I checked the corridor from the windows abutting our main door and did not find anyone there. So I went to the balcony and saw two women, who I thought were maids, standing near the car parking on the ground floor. I shouted to them for help, but from our fifth floor my voice didn't carry to them. So, I tried whistling to them to catch their attention."

"Ok..."

"That was the mistake I made, man. The first time they heard the whistle they looked at me but did not respond. Then, I whistled again and when they looked up I made signs asking them to come up. After that the women left the place and not knowing what to do I got back inside. I was thinking of ways to come out when suddenly someone started banging on the door. I went to the main door and saw from the window that two guys were kicking the door."

"Oh! Who were they?"

"That is what I am coming to. I noticed that the two women whom I whistled to were also present there. I opened the window to ask them to open the door and that was when I clearly heard what they were shouting at me. The women thought I was making lewd signs at them and they brought their husbands to get my ass whipped."

"Oh! And then? Those people would have noticed the lock on the door, right? Also how did they identify our house?" enquired Ravi.

"The women were working as maids in some apartment on our floor, so I think they recognised my face. Those people were so agitated that they did not care to look at the lock hanging on the door. The men created such ruckus there that one of our neighbours got scared and called the police."

"Police?" gasped Ravi.

“Yes. Fifteen minutes after that stuff started, two policemen entered the scene and that calmed down the gang which was abusing me. I explained the story to the policemen and they took the spare key from me and opened the door. Those people who attacked our house realised their mistake but did not relent fearing some action from the police. The women stood by their word that I made lewd remarks at them. One of them cooked up a new story. She told the police that I whistle to her daily. The policemen mediated and the gang left the place after giving me a warning that if I do something like this again, they will cut me to pieces,” Ganesh’s voice was trembling with fear.

“Oh!”

“Our neighbours took turns at our door to see what was happening. They looked at me like an animal in the zoo. I felt so ashamed that if at that time I found you there I would have murdered you,” Ganesh roared.

“I am extremely sorry, Ganesh. Please forgive me. I myself am in shock hearing what you said. How could something as simple as locking you inside the house, snowball into something this big?”

“That is not the end of the story. The policemen who came to the house said that they will take me to the police station.”

”What?” Ravi was shocked and asked, “but why?”

“I asked the same question and they said for creating nuisance.”

“Nuisance?”

“Yes, they said that they believed in whatever those women told them and that they will take me to the police station to interrogate me. I held their legs and begged them. After ten minutes, I realised why they were creating this scene.”

"Oh! They wanted money?" asked Ravi.

"Yes...they took 200 bucks from me, gave me a warning and then left the place. All because of you...you made me a donkey in front of everyone. Tonight I am gonna kick you for sure."

Ravi repeated the same line again, "Sorry Ganesh, sorry..."

"You thought that ended my troubles for the day. Because of this entire ruckus I was late to the office. It was almost 11:30 a.m. by the time I reached there. My manager gave me a stern warning and asked me to apply for half a day's leave."

"Oh!"

"Dude...today I will drink a Redbull and wait for you. Whatever time you come home, I don't care. You are gonna feel how powerful my punches are," saying this Ganesh hung the phone.

"Hello...hello..." Ravi's heart stopped for a moment and started beating again. Ganesh had a hefty personality and Ravi started fearing about what his condition would be if he gets beaten up by Ganesh.

But at present, he had a different problem to solve which was more important. He remembered that Praveen had called him to come and meet him. Taking his thoughts away from Ganesh, he tried to concentrate on the present issue at hand.

'This is the correct time for me to take him for a coffee. Will tell him that I was about to have a coffee and thought he would be interested in having one too.' Thinking this way Ravi first went to the coffee machine and filled two cups with coffee. He dropped the pills in the cup in his right hand and then walked to Praveen's room.

❖❖❖

Chapter 14

Executing the Plan

03:45 p.m.

Just as Ravi was about to approach Praveen's cabin, Suresh met him.

"Hi Ravi..."

"Hi..." replied Ravi but was irritated by the fact that Suresh had stopped him as he was about to put his plan into action.

"You said that I can meet you around 3 o'clock and discuss with you the changes that I did to the UI."

"Right! But Praveen asked me to meet him now. Kind of urgent, I think. Why don't we postpone it a bit?"

"Oh! Is it? But it will take me just five minutes to explain the changes to you. Why don't we meet now? I will tell Praveen about it." Suresh was about to open Praveen's cabin door.

"No..." shouted Ravi. "Not now, Suresh. I understand your enthusiasm on this matter but now we have some urgent stuff to discuss. I will meet you today for sure."

"But it will take me only five minutes..." Suresh protested again.

Suresh's five minutes always ended up as one hour meetings. Ravi was very much familiar with what would happen once a discussion started with Suresh. 'This fellow will not agree when I tell him that a particular change he did is not needed. It will take me considerable amount of time to convince him,' thought Ravi and said, "I will meet you before 7. I promise you, dude."

Suresh was satisfied with the assurance from Ravi and walked away.

'Phew! That was a close call. Now I should try my best to make Praveen drink the coffee...' thinking this way Ravi knocked on Praveen's cabin door and opened it.

"Come in..."

Ravi entered the room and noticed that Ashish was standing beside Praveen and explaining some technical stuff to him.

'Oh no! Why is Ashish present here?' thought Ravi and said, "Hey Praveen! You said you wanted to meet me?"

"Yeah, right! Wait for two minutes, I will finish my discussion with Ashish then we can continue."

"Ok," said Ravi and with some trepidation he made his move. "Praveen... I was bringing coffee for myself and thought you might be interested in drinking one too. So brought a cup for you... Sorry Ashish! I did not know you would be here. Shall I bring one for you too?" he asked

"Oh! Thanks," said Praveen and continued. "I just had my lunch at 2:45, so I am not in a mood to have coffee now. Ashish, you can take that cup if you are interested."

Ravi was shocked. He did not expect such a turn of events.

"Oh sure!" said Ashish and clutched on to the cup in Ravi's right hand. Such a quick action from Ashish made Ravi hold the cup harder. Ashish tried pulling it from Ravi's hand and seeing that Ravi was holding onto it firmly, he tried pulling it harder. But Ravi did not loosen his grasp on the cup. He was in a state where he did not know what he was doing. Praveen and Ashish had dealt him a big shock.

After tugging for a few times, Ashish said, "Don't you want to give it to me?" and smiled.

Ravi got back to his senses and understood what had happened. He felt embarrassed with his own behaviour and said, "Uh! Oh! Sorry...take it." He offered the cup to Ashish.

Ashish took the cup from Ravi's hand and said, "Thanks."

Ravi's plan had gone haywire. He had to find an alternate plan or else he would be missing his date tonight. Though he made his mind work faster than a computer, he couldn't hit upon any proper plan.

Meanwhile, Praveen finished his discussion with Ashish, who left the room sipping coffee unmindful of what was mixed in it. Praveen then turned towards Ravi and said, "Ravi...why didn't you come for the meeting with the test team?"

"I went out for lunch and so couldn't come back on time."

"You should try to attend meetings, Ravi. You shouldn't skip them like this." Praveen changed to a more important subject.

"So did you get time to go through the code and identify where you should make changes if we undertake the Silverlight related changes?"

"No...not yet. Still going through the code," Ravi lied.

"Ok. Why I called you was to tell you that Rajeev scheduled a meeting between you and Carl. It will start at 9 o'clock tonight. Be ready with your analysis by that time," said Praveen.

Ravi tried to find an excuse for not attending the meeting. "Praveen, I don't want to stay back late in the office."

"Why?" asked Praveen with a stern look on his face.

"Nine o'clock means I will have to take the office cab."

"Yes, right! I will sign your request. You can go by the cab," said Praveen.

"I am not comfortable with that option, Praveen. Yesterday I had a terrible experience with the cab driver."

"Why? What happened?"

"Yesterday I took the cab at 10 in the night. The driver maintained a steady speed of 120 kmph and was complaining that he had to slow down at traffic signals. It seems that when he was a lorry driver he used to drive like that for hours together."

Praveen laughed at that and said, "Is that a big issue? Ask him to drive slowly."

"It is not just this much, Praveen. When I told him that it was dangerous to drive at that speed, he laughed it off and told me that everything depends on fate. It seems the person was involved in an accident that happened at the Punjagutta junction two months ago. He told me that he had almost seen the God! But it seems that the Lord told him that he still had some more time on earth and sent him back. So he firmly concluded that everything depends on our fate. I was so frightened with what he told me that I vowed not to board an office cab again."

"Oh! Come on Ravi. You don't get to go with the same cab driver everyday. Just tell the vehicle coordinator and he will give proper instructions to these cab people."

But Ravi did not give up. "This is not the first time, Praveen. Once I had a driver who slept while he was driving."

Praveen did not listen to this argument too. "Things like these don't happen on a daily basis, Ravi. Not everyone is complaining," he said.

But Ravi did not relent. He cooked up a new story on the fly. He tried persuading his manager one more time. "I don't know about others, Praveen. But I have had many problems with these cab people. For example, there was one shocking episode where people on the road almost beat me up for the mistake of the driver. That night, the cab in which I was travelling met with a small accident near the Madhapur junction and my driver picked up a fight with a biker. A huge crowd gathered at the junction and in the melee that followed, the passersby tried to beat me and the driver. One fellow from the group tried to snatch my bag and wallet. From that day on, I started fearing our office cabs. So, is it possible for me to take that call from my home?"

"No, Ravi. Don't be childish. I will give proper instructions to the vehicle coordinator. If you don't feel like taking the cab, go by the RTC bus. Work is more important to us than comfort. You can go home by the RTC bus today, nothing will happen to you. You are attending that meeting from office. Ok then, you may leave," said Praveen ending the discussion while making his point very clear.

Ravi was dejected. He came out of the room. His plan to make Praveen drink that laxative laced coffee failed. The plan had not only misfired but backfired. Ashish had shouldered the burden of 25 test cases and if he falls ill today that burden will fall back on him. 'God! Why does Ashish always come in between and spoil my plans.' He started cursing Ashish. Not knowing what to do, Ravi proceeded towards Naresh's desk and greeted him.

"Hello Naresh."

"Hi..." said Naresh and in a hushed tone asked, "did you mix it?"

"Will you come out? I will tell you what happened."

"Ok..." said Naresh and locked his desktop. He followed Ravi with a lot of excitement.

Once they were in the corridor, Ravi told Naresh what had happened.

"Shit! What shall we do now?" said Naresh and started thinking. After five minutes, he came out with an idea. "Do this. Call Rajeev and ask him what the agenda for the meeting with Carl is. Ask him if Praveen is also required for the meeting. If he says no, tell him that since you are not someone who can take decisions on whether a particular feature can be in or out of the release, it might make sense to have Praveen included in the meeting. Also in the meantime, convince Naina to stay back for the meeting. At least we will be ensuring that Praveen will not take her out for the dinner," he said.

Ravi liked the idea but was not sure that it will work. Praveen can tell Rajeev that Ravi's decision on Silverlight will be final and he can stay away from the meeting. Else Praveen can tell Rajeev that he will attend the meeting from home. However, Ravi had no other option but to try. "Thanks," said Ravi and walked towards his cubicle.

Naresh said, "Hey, by the way did you check your mails after lunch today? That thread on cockroaches has just blown out of proportions." Naresh always kept immense interest in the SOS-Hyderabad mail threads. That alias he thought was a stress buster. So, today's thread had naturally caught his attention again. He was reading each and every reply in that mail thread with a lot of interest.

"I will check that later, right now I have to call Rajeev."

The beauty with Indian software engineers is that they are always awake. Whether it is India or America, a given Indian employee is available 24x7.

'I love Rajeev. He is available at most times during our daytime,' thought Ravi and dialled Rajeev's number.

"Hello."

"Hey, hi Rajeev. This is me, Ravi from SOS."

"Hi Ravi. How are things going on?"

"Yeah, we are making good progress on the project side."

"So, why did you call me now?"

"Just wanted to ask you about the 9 o'clock IST meeting with Carl. What is the exact agenda?"

"Just as what Praveen wrote in the mail. We will talk about the Silverlight requirement."

"Oh that's it, is it? Great! But I thought it might be great if Praveen also attends the meeting."

"Oh! Is he not attending the meeting?" Rajeev's voice showed a tinge of surprise.

"No, he is not. I think he is going to leave the decision to me and Carl."

"Ok! But still I would prefer if Praveen attends it."

Ravi wanted to jump up with joy. 'Rajeev also wants Praveen to attend the meeting! That is great,' thought Ravi and said, "Yeah, even I would. Because I can just give the technical details on the subject, but managing schedules and other stuff is in his hands, right. So..."

"Yeah, true...I will write to him asking him to attend the meeting. Anything else..."

"No, nothing in particular."

"Ok then...see you in the meeting." Rajeev ended the call.

'Great! Now I will have to convince Naina to stay back for the meeting,' thought Ravi and was about to get up from his desk to meet her when he saw Ashish packing his bag and leaving for the day.

"Hi Ashish. What happened? You are leaving so early?" enquired Ravi.

"I have a severe stomach upset, Ravi. I wrote a mail to Praveen that I will be on leave for the rest of the day."

Ravi wanted to sound a bit courteous and said, "If you are not well Ashish, shall I take those 25 tests back?"

"No! I think I should be fine by tomorrow. I will come and work on them. Tomorrow, I will tell you whether I can complete them or not. For now, they are still my work item."

"Ok...as you wish. Take care of yourself. Get well soon," said Ravi, and Ashish walked away.

'It is good that Ashish still wants to work on those 25 test cases.' It was great news for Ravi because till that moment he was shivering, thinking about how he would be handling such a sudden increase in workload.

He approached Naina and greeted her, "Hi Naina..."

"Hi Ravi."

"You remember that Praveen asked me to meet Carl tonight, right?"

"Yes, I do."

"Since you are also working on the UI, I thought it might be a great idea if you could stay back for the meeting."

"Even I was thinking about that," said Naina.

'It is too good to be true,' thought Ravi. Both Rajeev and Naina are in agreement with him. So with a tinge of joy, Ravi said, "Yeah...since it has been just a week that you joined our team, it might be a good idea for you to get involved in a new work item like this. You will be able to understand the project better."

"Ok, I will stay back for the meeting. By the way it means that our dinner programme for today is cancelled, right? Did you inform others about it?" said Naina.

"Yes, I informed them. I told them that we can do this outing sometime later. We can go tomorrow or on the weekend," said Ravi.

"Great. I think weekend is a nice idea. We can cover more places. Even I am not in a mood to roam around the city with so much work to complete in two days," said Naina.

"Ok then...tell me if you need any help with those test cases."

"Yeah, sure."

"Bye then..." and Ravi walked back to his desk. He felt elated at the fact that he had put an alternate plan into motion.

❖❖❖

Chapter 15

03:20 p.m.

Dinner Plans

"Hello Praveen. This is Rajeev here."

"Hello. Hi Rajeev. What is the matter?"

"Ravi called me just now and told me that you are not attending the meeting with Carl. I thought it might be a good idea for you to stay back for the meeting."

'Ravi! Damn! He is doing too much,' thought Praveen and said, "hmm...I thought Ravi can handle the issue himself and I am not needed for the meeting, Rajeev. I think it is time we let Ravi get involved in making decisions about whether a feature is required or not. He and Carl can make their final decision."

"No, Praveen. It is not just about Silverlight. Your mail talked about introducing Silverlight into our schedule at a very late stage. It might affect our schedules too. It is better that you stay back and get involved in the meeting. I don't think Ravi can handle that well. Also you have signed up for some minor changes, right. You will be required to discuss about them too."

Praveen thought about different ways to get out of it but couldn't think of any. Finally he agreed, a little reluctantly though. "Ok...I will attend the meeting."

"Bye."

"Bye Rajeev." Praveen started cursing Ravi. 'Ravi thinks he has outwitted me? I will show him who can think better. I will ask Naina to also stay back and both of us can go to Domino's.'

He went to Naina's desk and told her that he was staying back for the night and it would be better if she stayed back too.

"Even I was planning to stay back," said Naina.

"Good. Let's go to Domino's at Indranagar for dinner."

"Ok..."

"Ok then...carry on with your work," said Praveen and he got back to his cabin.

As Ravi's cubicle was just opposite to Naina, he overheard the conversation and thought, 'Oh! Praveen also has the same plan of taking her to Domino's for dinner. What to do now?' But however hard he thought, he couldn't hit upon an idea. Finally, he decided to take Naresh's help again.

He went to his cubicle and said, "Naresh, can you come out with me for a second. Have some problem..."

Naresh was busy with something and he said, "What is the problem, dude? I am busy right now."

"You know what it is about? Now come out, it is just a five minute discussion."

Naresh reluctantly got up and followed Ravi to the corridor.

"What are you busy with? I thought you are the only developer who is done with almost everything for the current release," Ravi enquired.

"Oh that!" Naresh smiled and said, "the mails in the SOS-Hyderabad alias. They are super-interesting. I was going through them."

"What? What is so interesting about those mails?"

"That cockroach mail in the afternoon, it snowballed into a

completely different discussion, dude. Haven't you read any of those mails?" asked Naresh.

"No...right now I am not interested in that discussion. I am more interested in finding a solution to this issue."

Talking to each other, they reached an empty corridor and Naresh asked him, "What is your problem this time?"

"I have managed to make Praveen and Naina stay back for the meeting. But Praveen is planning to take Naina to Domino's for dinner. What should I do?"

"Can't you think of a solution for such a silly issue, Ravi." Naresh was a bit irritated with the way Ravi was constantly approaching him for answers.

"Dude! My mind is not working from the time I knew that Praveen is my competitor. I am in a big confusion today. Also one of my friends told me today how he got fired for fighting with his boss, so I don't know how to walk that tight rope without getting Praveen agitated about it."

"Ok...this is the last time I give you some advice on this subject. Next time think for yourself. For now the only thing that I can think about it is, when you see Praveen taking Naina out for the dinner, ask them if you can join them. It is not some private occasion to give a special dinner to Naina, so Praveen will most probably agree to that."

"What if he does not?"

"Hmm...in that case you know that they are going to Domino's, right?"

"Yeah, right."

"Then, when you see them leave for Domino's, ask Suresh to join you for dinner. Take him to Domino's and there you can tell them how surprised you are to see them there. The main idea is to make it a team dinner instead of a date."

"Great idea!" shouted Ravi. "You are so helpful, Naresh. You are my best friend." Ravi started praising Naresh.

Naresh was elated to hear Ravi praising him so much and said, "No problem, dude. It is my duty to help you as a friend. Anyway, best of luck." And both of them started walking back to their desks.

On the one hand, Praveen was happy that he had successfully misled Ravi into believing that he was taking Naina to Domino's, but on the other hand, he was getting restless. 'How can Ravi make me stay back for the night? Am I his boss? Or is he my boss? Who told him to call Rajeev? It is time I give him a shock in front of the whole team, especially before Naina.' Praveen opened his Outlook and started typing a mail. The mail was addressed to all his reports and it read...

Hi team,

Since Friday is just two days away. I thought it will be a nice idea to schedule a status update meeting at 4:30 p.m. in my room for the next two days. Please assemble in my room at 4:30 p.m.

Regards,

Praveen

'Now I will show Ravi his place,' thought Praveen and clicked on 'Send Message'.

After Naresh had finished giving Ravi his advice, Naresh again got back to his original topic of the cockroach mail. "Ravi! That thread is hilarious, you know. The discussion has changed into something else completely. If you get some time, look at it dude..." and he started laughing.

Repeated references by Naresh to the mail thread also made Ravi enthusiastic about what was happening in the thread. The first thing he did as soon as he sat at his desk was to open the SOS-Hyderabad folder. That mail thread had become huge with hundred odd replies to the original mail, and he started reading mails randomly from the list.

The fight between the employees had continued for a while when someone wrote this mail.

'There are lots of cockroaches at my home too. How to get rid of this menace?'

When it comes to an IT company, it is full of people who are well-trained to find answers to any problem. And true to their credentials, there were around five people who replied with solutions. Some homemade and some suggesting some sprays in the market. And an enquiry followed it.

Someone suggested that the... *'Spray is effective in killing cockroaches. The same company advertises that the spray is effective against rats. Is it true? Recently while cleaning my cupboards I noticed a rat running in my house, so I would like to use this spray based on your feedback.'*

Someone replied to this mail with his own solution.

"Yeah, rats are a big problem. At my home, they ate away our electric wires and made big holes in our cupboards. The spray you told about is ineffective. You must have seen the recent TV ad from the... company which sells rat poison... it is very effective. You can use it. ..."

Seeing those mails, Ravi thought, 'The outside world thinks that software engineers work on complicated problems and write code which changes the world! While herein they discuss about rats and cockroaches.'

Ravi continued reading the mail thread.

The next reply said...

"Rat poison is useless as well as dangerous. Use the traditional method of using rat traps. You get them for cheap at Indranagar which is very near to our office..."

To this, the person who vouched for the rat poison replied...

"Rat traps? That is a joke...I tried them and I couldn't even catch one..."

And this started a fight...

'That is a joke'.

I sincerely tried to give my opinion on this aspect and your remarks hurt me... I hope you don't repeat it again. Also, I tried using rat poison at home but got scared at the prospect of my child getting in touch with it, so I reverted to using traps for catching rats.

'I tried them and I couldn't even catch one'.

This means you don't know how to use one..."

The reply to this mail was instant...

"Could you please tell me how I offended you? I just said rat traps are ineffective when there are lots of mice running around. Anyway the way you said, 'This means you don't know how to use one...' was clearly offending."

Meanwhile, some other overenthusiastic reader tried to share his knowledge with the community.

"My 2 cents... You have to bargain well when you purchase rat traps from the vendor at Indranagar. I bought it for Rs 100 and my friend managed to buy it for Rs 50 . Make sure that you don't wear your 'SOS' tag, when you go for shopping in that area... They overprice the stuff if they know you are a software guy."

The next reply changed the track of the discussions again.

"On a funny note... Why not buy a cat? Addresses two issues...

a. You get a pet.

b. It will eliminate the rats."

Just as Ravi was about to go to the next mail, he noticed a new mail from Praveen in his inbox. It was the mail informing team about the status updates at 4:30 p.m.

'Another status update meeting! Is Praveen out of his mind? We did a couple of status updates in the morning and why this status update meeting again?' But Ravi did not realise the fact that the meeting was for him.

❖❖❖

Chapter 16

An Unexpected Turn

04:15 p.m.

It was still 4:15 p.m. and Ravi still had fifteen minutes before the meeting in Praveen's room was to start. So, he got back to his work and started debugging his code. He was hardly done with fixing one test case when his internal office messenger flashed a message from Praveen.

'It is time for the status update meeting. Assemble in my room.'

As usual, Ravi got irritated with the disturbance which happened when he was about to finish completing some work. Reluctantly he got up and went to Praveen's cabin. There he noticed that the others had already assembled.

"Praveen, we already did a couple of updates in the morning, right? Why this update again?" asked Naresh.

"Hmm...I thought it might be a good idea to know the status once in the morning and once in the evening because this way I will be able to track the progress over the next two days better. Also, it is on Friday evening that we are supposed to be submitting the code. Hence, it is better if we have one meeting in the evening too."

This time Praveen started the meeting with Naresh and proceeded to the others. He kept Ravi's update to the end as he wanted to take his time with Ravi. After finishing with all the members, he finally arrived at Ravi.

"Ravi, what is your update?"

"I fixed two more bugs. Done with eight in all. Two more remaining."

"What about the test cases?"

"Finished 25. Took ten more. Did two from the morning. Gave 25 to Ashish."

"What? You completed only two tests since the morning?"

"Because of all the meetings I could get only two hours to work..." Ravi tried to explain.

"What meetings? All of us attended the meetings, right? How come the others registered better progress than you?"

When someone asks such questions, it is difficult to even think of an answer. Without trying to draw any comparisons with others, Ravi tried walking the tight line. "The volume of my work is high this time and the tests are also complicated, so I could write only one test per hour."

Suresh interrupted here. "Oh is it! I went through your code yesterday and I thought writing tests for UI was simple." Though the statement was put in the most polite manner it could have ever been, it had its desired effect on Ravi.

He wanted to shout at Suresh but toned down his reply and tried to be polite. But, however polite he wanted to be, his reply was harsh enough to indicate his unpleasantness with Suresh. "No Suresh...it isn't. I am the owner of that code segment and I know what is easy and what is complicated."

But Suresh was a person who always tried to show the others in the team that he did his homework well. So he replied, "Maybe you are correct but when I was going through your test cases yesterday, I thought most of them followed the same template. Hence, I thought they were easy."

‘What! He went through my tests too?’ Ravi was getting restless with the discussion and Praveen was thoroughly enjoying it.

Ravi tried to defend his position and said, “Some of the tests that we wrote in the beginning followed the same template. But the ones that I am writing now are different. They take time.”

Suresh said, “Ok...” and put an expression on his face which indicated that he was not happy with Ravi’s answer.

It was here that Praveen entered the discussion again. “They might have been complicated, Ravi. But two tests since the morning is too less. What did you do since the morning?”

‘Even my dad never asked me such questions and here my manager is making such statements. I think I understand what he is trying to do...’ thought Ravi and tried answering that question from Praveen. He explained to him how his time got wasted in the meetings, how he was able to work on the bugs in the morning and how the tests were getting complicated. But even after listening to all that, Praveen seemed not too happy about his progress. “I am not happy with the way things are going on, Ravi. You should try to complete your tasks faster,” saying this Praveen then moved onto something else.

With each such statement from Praveen, Ravi’s blood pressure was shooting up. ‘I am working hard for the completion of my items and still my manager keeps prodding me like this. I hope there will be a time when I become the manager and Praveen my report. I will show him what I am capable of doing.’ But this is what most people might call ‘wishful thinking’.

“Ravi! Did you look at the production issue which was reported in the afternoon?”

Ravi stammered on this and said, “No...I did not look at that issue. Ashish said he would be looking into it, so I thought I can concentrate on my work.”

That was what Praveen was waiting for. "How can you say that, Ravi? A critical component goes down and you don't even try to find a solution to it? Ashish is unwell and has left for home; no one is working on that issue now. At least show some interest in reading mails on such critical failures. Will you look into it now?" asked Praveen.

Ravi was already feeling choked with work and this new addition to that ever increasing list of work items was making him feel really uncomfortable. Since he was the senior-most developer in the project, he was expected to take responsibility for such fixes. But this meant he should skip dinner and work the whole night. Ravi was thinking, 'How do I handle this issue?' when suddenly Suresh responded. "Praveen...I have looked into that issue. I even discussed the fix with Ashish before he left for the day. It is a simple fix. I can do it in a couple of hours."

Till that moment Ravi felt Suresh was his enemy, but now he felt Suresh was his saviour. 'Without him I would have been dead today. I love Suresh...' he thought.

The intervention from Suresh was a big surprise for Praveen. He had planned to burden Ravi with so much work that he was expecting to see him withdraw from the race, being unable to face the attack. But Suresh had spoiled his plans for the evening. Still Praveen did not want to loosen his hold on Ravi and tried to convince Suresh.

"No Suresh...I think this item is better handled by Ravi. He has been working on this project for the last two years and he knows the code segments well. Since it is a production issue, I don't want any bugs on this later. Better leave it to him."

Ravi got scared seeing how Praveen was manipulating the situation to his own favour. But before Ravi could utter anything, Suresh protested, "I have already fixed this issue. I am just writing the test cases. I have already discussed the fix with Ashish who agreed that my fix is correct. All the previous tests are passing too. I will do it..."

Ravi seized the opportunity and said, "Yeah...if it is working fine then let him take it, Praveen. Why waste my time on it again? I have lots of other items to finish."

Praveen did not find any valid reason to counter that argument and finally agreed. He told the team that the status update meeting was over and asked Naresh and Suresh to leave. He asked Naina and Ravi to stay back, so that they could talk about UI progress.

After the door closed Praveen enquired, "Ravi, I think our progress on the UI related work items is very poor. At this rate, do you think can we even meet the Friday deadline?"

Ravi was surprised as well as shocked to see his manager talking like that. "I already told you Praveen that we are on track. I can meet the deadline. We are done with all the priority '0' test cases. Only the lower priority items are remaining. Even if we slip, I will work on the weekend and complete them."

Praveen expressed his displeasure and said, "You know since a long time that Friday is the deadline then how can you be so careless, Ravi."

"I...I..." Ravi was shivering with fear. He did not know how this stuff was going to affect his review. But at the same time he knew that the argument of Praveen held little water. 'We still have two days for the deadline and he can scold me if I don't meet that deadline. What is this now?' thought Ravi.

"I think Naina is doing her best to learn the project. I am more worried about the progress you are making. As a senior developer, the expectations are high from you. You are not living up to those expectations, Ravi. At this rate, it is getting difficult for me to project your achievements to my higher ups too."

"But Praveen, there are still two days for the deadline. I will try to meet that deadline. You need not worry too much."

"See...this attitude of yours is what holds you back from growing in the organisation, Ravi."

"What attitude?"

"Even now you are saying that you will 'try' to meet the deadline. You should confidently tell me that you 'will' meet the deadline. This attitude of yours is what bothers me the most."

Ravi thought, 'What the hell! It is pure harassment. But why is he pricking me so much. Is it just to tell me that I should keep away from the girl he loves or is there something else?' But he kept quiet as there was no other way to tackle such mindless dialogue.

Praveen's next statement was what helped Ravi understand the true purpose of the meeting.

"Ravi, I think you are unable to take this extra burden of helping Naina. Let me do one thing. From tomorrow, I will take the task of helping her. What do you say, Naina?"

Naina did not know what politics were going on between Ravi and Praveen. Neither did she care for that. She did not even know that Praveen was being too harsh with Ravi. Being new to the corporate world, she thought this was how projects were dealt with. But for courtesy sake, she said, "Ravi was very helpful. He has helped me very well till now."

"I know he helps others well. But I think that is affecting his work. So from tomorrow onwards, I will take the knowledge transfer sessions. Ok then Ravi, you can concentrate on your own work from tomorrow," said Praveen. It was a sign from Praveen that he has firmly decided about the change.

'He is trying to cut the professional relation between me and Naina. He wants to be closer to her,' Ravi thought. But what else can he do to counter what his manager had decided to do. So with a very heavy heart Ravi agreed, "Okay Praveen, as you say so..."

"Ok good. Now you can leave. Try to make more progress by tomorrow's scrum time, Ravi," said Praveen and ended the conversation.

❖❖❖

Chapter 17

A Confession

05:00 p.m.

It was the third time today that Ravi was coming out depressed from Praveen's cabin. He started fearing that room. 'Maybe there is a *Vastu* problem with that room. Every time I enter it, I come out depressed. Something is wrong with it.' This time Ravi felt even worse because Praveen was using every available opportunity to make Ravi an ass before Naina.

The way Praveen had dealt with him in the status update meeting made him feel so bad that the only way he thought he could come out of it was by sharing his miserable story with someone else. And that 'someone else' was none other than Naresh again.

"Hey."

"Hi... What did he say?"

"What else would he say? Care to come with me for snacks?"

"Ok..." and both of them left for the cafeteria.

"So? What did he say?" Naresh asked again.

"These daily fights with him have made me a bit thick-skinned, otherwise today I would have been crying."

"What did he do now?"

"He said he wanted to take over the task of explaining the UI code to Naina. He said that I am falling behind schedule because of that extra burden."

"Ok. That is good news I think, right? You have less work to worry about."

"Less work is good news but at the same time Praveen did it so that he can get closer to Naina and push me out of the equation. Not just that dude, the things he called me in the meeting, it was all a predetermined plot to defame me in front of her."

"Don't be so silly. Girls won't be so much influenced about whether you are prompt with your office work or not." Naresh gave a small five minute lecture to Ravi on what girls expect from guys, how Ravi should try to woo Naina, how he should introduce himself to her, what gifts to give her, how to address her etc.

But Ravi wasn't listening to all that. With each passing moment, he was getting more and more agitated. "He said my attitude is not correct. I don't take extra responsibility. I don't complete work on time. I don't plan well. Whatever came to his mouth he said all that..."

"Oh! Is it? Just forget about it, dude. Even during normal times we get to hear all that crap. Now that you are competing with him on something, the tone is going to get harsher. In the morning you were prepared for all that, right?"

"Yeah, right! But it is becoming too much. This way I will quit from the company in another month, I cannot bear it anymore."

"Hey! Don't behave so stupidly. Never take such hasty decisions. You think you will get a super-boss if you change companies?"

"Maybe you are correct, but at least my pay would increase."

"This is recession time, dude. The other company will make you an offer and most probably give you the same salary as you get here. What is the use?"

"Is it?"

"Yes, one of my friends jumped companies and they offered him the same salary that he was getting in his previous company. And when he asked them the reason for that, they told him to be happy with the fact that he was at least being offered a job."

That fact made Ravi change his decision. "Oh! Then better I stay here. But the fact that even Suresh tries to meddle with my affairs is making me feel bad about my overall experience at SOS."

"Yeah, I saw the way he tried to make you a fool in that meeting. He tried that once with me too and after that he stopped it."

"Why did he stop it?"

"If you remember well, he tried to overact in the first week that he joined our project. After that for around two weeks, I made sure that his mistakes were highlighted everyday in the scrum."

"Yeah, right! I thought you were doing it so that he could learn about the project well. Didn't think it was some revenge tactic."

Naresh laughed and said, "After that he never tried to meddle in my affairs. Now that you are a soft target, he is trying to show his prowess on you. Now you too try something like what I did and he will keep quiet."

"Ok...looks like a good idea."

"But the way Praveen treats me...I sometimes feel he thinks that I am a worthless individual. These days he is calling me something or the other every day."

"If he is bothering you so much why don't you complain to the HR or to Ramnath?"

"If you promise me that you will not tell anyone. I will tell you something."

"What is it?"

"Two months ago, I complained to Ramnath about Praveen's behaviour. I told him how he was ill-treating me. Ramnath was very attentive and told me that he will look into the issue. I thought some action would be taken against Praveen but as you see now, nothing has happened. They are friends dude, complaining is of no use."

Naresh was surprised with Ravi's confession. "I never thought you had so much courage, dude. Why don't you try the HR route this time?"

"Do you really think going to the HR will be useful? Ramnath and Praveen are friends. HR will in turn question my attitude. Also, I don't have any proof to show them that he is torturing me on a daily basis."

"Dude! If you ask me for advice, my suggestion is to forget about all this and concentrate on your work. There is no point discussing about matters like these. It is very difficult to bell these cats," telling this Naresh laughed.

"I am not asking for your advice, dude. I was just sharing my thoughts with you. Sometimes I feel like setting up my own firm. Why should I work with managers like these?"

"Do you think setting up your own business is an easy thing?"

"I don't think it is easy. But I was thinking that it might be more satisfying to set up my own business and slog than to get thrashed by someone like Praveen on a daily basis."

"Doing your own business is a risky thing dude. One of my friends tried his hand at this thing and burnt his fingers badly."

"What happened?"

"He partnered with one of his very close friend and that fellow finally ditched him by stealing around one lakh rupees?"

"What? But he might not have chosen his partner correctly."

"Dude! There is nothing like correct or incorrect here. It is all about money. Both of them had been friends since their senior secondary days. Do you expect someone whom you had known for such a long time to ditch you like that?"

"Oh! That means, when it comes to business I cannot trust close friends like you too," joked Ravi and smiled.

"Yeah...if you ask me...I have lost interest in all this kind of business deals with anyone after what happened to my friend. They are too risky and not worth the effort."

"But someday I will establish my own business, dude. Just that someone failed miserably doesn't mean that I will fail too. I will choose someone better."

"Maybe...but the kind of tensions you will have to face will be immense, dude. We have a happy life here. Me, my PC and my project. Outside this company, you will always be worried about where you are spending your money, who is spending your money, are you getting cheated etc. And if yours is an SME, you will always be earning something similar to your pay package here. Don't get carried away by the stories of Infosys or Microsoft, dude. Not all companies end up like them."

"It was just a thought, dude. I don't even know whether I will ever put up my own firm. But sometimes when I talk to people like Praveen and Suresh, I tend to think I am better off doing my own stuff compared to working with them." The thought of Praveen brought a sad look on Ravi's face. Noticing the change, Naresh tried to change the topic.

"Hey leave Praveen, dude. Does thinking about him or about what he did to you decrease your sadness? If you ask me, today there is awesome stuff going on in that mail thread."

"What mail thread?"

"Oh! You forgot again? I was talking about that thread which started during lunch time."

"Ok...that one, is it? I was halfway through that when Praveen called us for the meeting."

"Ok...till what point did you read?" asked Naresh.

Ravi understood that Naresh was getting ready to tell him what the mails in the thread were. But he was in no mood to listen to all that crap again. He had more important issues to concentrate on. He decided to divert the topic and was searching for ideas when he saw Deepa enter the cafeteria.

Ravi put his hand on Naresh's shoulder and said, "Leave that topic aside. There are more important issues for us here. You noticed her?"

"Who?"

"Your girlfriend!" joked Ravi.

"Who? Deepa is it? Where?" Ravi noticed the excitement in Naresh's voice. Naresh had already started looking all around the place for her and finally, he found her sitting at one of the corner tables and chatting with someone.

The presence of Deepa always made Naresh forget about his surroundings. He started gazing at her with admiration, forgetting about the fact that Ravi was beside him.

Ravi tried to tease him. "Naresh," he said, but Naresh was apparently not listening to anything and did not respond to Ravi's call. He was still gazing at Deepa and was smiling to himself.

Ravi shouted this time, "Naresh!" to which he responded.

"Huh... Yeah, what?"

"Who are you so keenly looking at, dude?" asked Ravi.

"Who? No one...I was just looking at the chocolates in the counter."

"Yeah, I know what chocolate you were looking at."

Naresh got embarrassed with that statement and as usual got angry. "Stop it, okay. I will look at whatever I want to. Why should you be bothered about that?"

Ravi tried to calm him down and said, "I am not bothered about anything. Just wanted to tell you that if you are really interested in her then go ahead and talk to her? Why sit here and waste your time?"

That statement had the desired effect and Naresh cooled down. He sighed and said, "Do you think she will talk to me?"

"Yeah surely, she will," Ravi exuded confidence.

It was just ten minutes ago that Naresh gave Ravi all sorts of advices on how to deal with girls. But when it came to himself, his mind stopped working. "But what will I tell her?" he asked.

Ravi thought for a second and said, "Remind her about that team outing. She met you there, right?"

Naresh smiled and jumped up with excitement. "Good idea! You are really smart, Ravi," he said.

"Thanks for the compliments. Now go and talk to her."

Naresh got up from his seat but fear gripped him again. He couldn't muster the courage to talk to her and sat back in his chair.

Ravi was enjoying himself with all that was happening and again goaded Naresh. “Go Naresh. Don’t be so timid. Go and talk to her.”

“Why don’t you come with me?” asked Naresh.

“What? Me? Why?”

“Yeah, this idea is good. She will not get doubtful if both of us meet her. Come on, come with me,” he said.

“No way, I am not coming,” said Ravi.

Naresh begged Ravi, tried to scold him into submission and then even threatened to beat him, but none of that worked.

“This is your love story, dude. Not mine. If you are interested, go and meet her otherwise let’s sit here and talk about something else,” Ravi sounded defiant.

Again Naresh got up and took two steps forward, but he felt he did not have the required confidence to go and meet her. He begged Ravi again. “Dude! I gave you so many ideas since morning and still you are ditching me like this?”

Ravi did not relent and said, “If you think you cannot go there, let’s get back to our cubicles. Why waste time here?”

Cursing Ravi, Naresh started walking towards Deepa’s table. Ravi was super-excited with what was happening before him. He gazed intently at Naresh and Deepa.

Naresh approached Deepa’s table and found that she was still busy discussing something with another person, who apparently was her teammate.

Naresh waited for the discussion to end and finally mustered enough courage to talk to her. He cleared his throat in a loud way which attracted the attention of both Deepa and her teammate.

“Hi Deepa, I was just passing by and wanted to say hello to you,” he said.

“Well. Hi, but who are you?” she questioned Naresh.

Naresh’s heart stopped for a second. He hadn’t expected such a blunt reply from her but still he held onto the idea given by Ravi.

“You don’t remember me? You remember the outing that our teams had two months ago.”

Deepa thought for a second and said, “Yeah, right. I remember. You are from that supermarket team, right?”

“Yes, you are very sharp. You recollect well,” Naresh tried to flatter her.

“Well. Thank you for that. So, you need some assistance,” asked Deepa.

“Assistance? For what?” asked Naresh.

“I thought you came to me for some help, otherwise why anyone would greet me all of a sudden.”

Naresh started thinking hard for a reason and finally hit upon some excuse. “Yes, you are right. I just wanted to know if there are any openings in your team. I am planning to move.”

“Well, if there are any I will mail it to you. Just tell me your email ID,” she said. Naresh eagerly gave her his mail ID, turned towards Ravi and winked at him showing that he had achieved something.

‘Naresh really knows how to tackle girls. She is already taking some information,’ thought Ravi. At the very same moment, Deepa looked at Ravi and noticed that he was intensely gazing her.

Under her breath she said, “Stupid,” which Naresh heard.

He thought she meant him by that and enquired, “Uh! What?”

“No...it is not about you. You see that person sitting there,” saying this Deepa pointed her finger towards Ravi, who also turned around to see whom those people were pointing to. “He is ogling me since a very long time. I don’t know where these people recruit such people from,” she said.

“Yeah, true. That is disgusting,” said Naresh and a new idea struck him. “I will talk to him. Don’t worry,” he said.

“No...don’t take so much trouble. Leave him,” said Deepa.

“These people should be taught how to behave. I will talk to him. You continue your discussion, Deepa. By the way thanks for helping me,” said Naresh and swiftly moved towards Ravi.

It was now Deepa’s turn to see what Naresh was up to. She noticed that Naresh reached Ravi’s place, said something to him, caught him by the collar and pulled him out of her sight.

‘Wow,’ thought Deepa and turned to her teammate and continued her discussion with him.

What Naresh actually did was, he reached Ravi’s place told him that Deepa thought Ravi was ogling her and asked him not to react to anything that he was doing. So, Ravi did not say anything as Naresh caught him by the collar and pulled him out.

After reaching a safe place Naresh asked Ravi, “What do you think she would have thought about me?”

“I think you would have made a positive impression. You think well, dude,” he complimented.

“Today I am lucky,” said Naresh and looked to be in a highly jubilant mood. “By the way, thanks for the help.”

“Anything for my friend,” Ravi said and looked at his watch. It showed 5:45 p.m. He remembered the 7:00 p.m. dinner plan. “Naresh...it is around 6:00 now. I have some work to finish before that meeting with Carl in the night. Shall we go now?”

“Oh! Is it 5:45 already? I have to catch the company bus at 6. Good that you told me.”

Both of them got up and walked towards the lifts.

❖❖❖

Chapter 18

The Dinner Decision

06:45 p.m.

Finally, after a very long time Ravi could work uninterruptedly for an hour. He was happy that he was finally able to make a good progress with his work when suddenly Suresh appeared at his desk.

'What the...! Why is he here now?' thought Ravi and putting a smile on his face asked, "Why are you here?"

"You said that you would meet me before 7:00 p.m. today. It is already 6:45, so thought you might want to do that meeting now."

'Given a chance I would never want to do that meeting,' thought Ravi. But having no other option he had to agree to that proposal now. "Ok...tell me what changes you did to the solution."

Suresh was happy that finally he got a chance to show his excellent work to someone. He started with the image change. "I changed the image on the welcome screen."

"Yeah, I know that. When you mentioned about this change in the scrum, Sudeep and Praveen did not agree to that, right?"

"They may not have but I still think that it is not the correct image that they used. I wanted to discuss it with you again."

"No, Suresh. That thing is fixed. We did that after contacting our customer. Carl won't be happy if we deviate from that decision."

"Whatever the customers might say, that need not be the final word, right? Why don't we convince him to agree to do the correct thing?"

"Correct thing? Changing that image is your decision, Suresh. You cannot decide what is correct or incorrect. It is up to the customer to decide what is the correct thing for him."

"No...I still cannot believe that a middle-aged lady carrying a kid would make good impression on viewers. It is not trendy. I doubt if it will attract any hits."

"That is the customer's decision, Suresh. Maybe they want to target the family audience. Sudeep already had a long discussion with Carl on this. Also most supermarket pages are like that," Ravi made some statement off the cuff.

"Most supermarket webpages? Can you show me some examples?"

The question irritated Ravi the most. 'Wherefrom I will get an example for him now?' Controlling his anger Ravi said, "As of now, I don't have any examples with me. But if you insist on seeing an example then I will try to find one."

"But that means there is no ready answer available for questions like these. Why don't we talk to Carl and try to understand the issue better?"

'Bullshit! Just two days to meet our deadline and we are talking about changes like these. It is the limit for craziness,' thought Ravi. Given a chance, he wanted to spank Suresh like a kid. But neither Suresh was a kid, nor was violence allowed at office. So showing patience, Ravi said, "You can discuss it with Carl but take Praveen's permission first. If you ask me for my opinion then I will not sign up for something like this, that too when our deadline is so near."

That answer was not to Suresh's satisfaction. So he tried arguing, "I think we should be more bothered about the quality of our work and the impact it has on customers and not about meeting deadlines."

'Does he know what he is talking about? Is he trying to be childish? Is he saying that I am not bothered about the quality? Or is he saying that we should accept the changes that he is suggesting?' These questions were heating up Ravi's mind. He did not want to get into an argument with Suresh and mess up with him before leaving for the dinner. Fortunately for Ravi, at that very moment Praveen walked to Naina's desk.

Ravi heard Praveen asking Naina for dinner. "Shall we go for dinner?" asked Praveen.

"Ok..." said Naina.

To catch their attention, Ravi took his gaze away from Suresh and smiled at Naina and Praveen. Looking at the two of them, Naina felt that it would be good manners if she asked Ravi and Suresh to join them for dinner.

"Guys, do you want to join us for dinner?" asked Naina.

That statement gave Praveen a jolt. 'What the...' He hadn't planned to invite them for dinner. But being the team manager it wouldn't be appropriate if he didn't invite them for dinner himself. So he said, "Yeah...forgot to ask you people. Will you join us for dinner?"

Listening to that, Ravi was overjoyed. But before he could say 'yes', Suresh chipped in and said, "No...I am full. Also we are busy discussing my changes to the UI. You go ahead."

Praveen snatched the opportunity and said, "Ok...then you proceed with your discussion."

Ravi felt like slapping Suresh. But before Praveen could leave, controlling his anger he said, “Praveen...I am hungry. I can join you for the dinner. We can do this discussion in the restaurant.”

Praveen replied, “Ok...but since Suresh is saying that this discussion is important let’s do one thing. I will get both of you a pizza each. You can have your dinner here. What say?”

“Nice idea,” said Suresh. Praveen congratulated himself for his quick thinking.

‘Bullshit!’ thought Ravi and his mind started racing for more ideas. Finally, he hit upon the perfect idea.

“No, Praveen. I think we will join you for the dinner at the restaurant. Suresh had some questions here which he wanted to discuss with you before putting them to Carl. So, it is better if we have this discussion at the restaurant. Both you and I can debate about the changes that Suresh has done.”

This solution made Suresh happy. “Yeah Praveen, I think it is a good idea. Even I will come to the restaurant. I have some stuff to discuss with you.”

Praveen’s happiness evaporated into thin air. He thought hard and finally said, “But Suresh might need to demonstrate the changes on the computer here. So if you people come to the restaurant, it might not be so intuitive for us to understand what the changes are.”

Suresh agreed with Praveen’s point, “Yeah, you are right. What shall we do then?” After thinking for a minute, Suresh said, “Ok Praveen, in that case you can leave for the restaurant. I will continue this discussion with Ravi.”

Praveen felt as if a big burden was put off his chest. It was Ravi’s turn to think hard, but his mind could not find any great idea and he started cursing Suresh for putting him in a soup. Right at that moment Naina saved him.

"Let's do one thing. We can call Domino's, order pizzas and have them delivered to our office. We can have our dinner here. That will save us time. I still have my test cases to complete and am not really in a mood to waste time."

Listening to her statement, Ravi's face lit up. "Yes...that is a very good idea, Naina! Let's order them here. It solves all the problems," he said.

Suresh liked the idea too. "Yeah...nice idea," he said.

Praveen could not think of anything which could counter the argument and agreed reluctantly. "Ok...who is going to give the order then?" he asked.

"I will do it," said Naina.

"Praveen, can you join us for the discussion while she is giving the order?" asked Ravi.

Praveen was upset with the way his dinner plan was reduced to ashes. He was not in a mood to participate in any meeting and said, "Right now I am a bit busy, I will join you guys in half an hour." Saying this he got back to his cabin.

Ravi looked at the watch and it showed 7:15 p.m. He still had to bear with Suresh for another two hours before they could attend Carl's meeting and call the day off. Ravi was getting both bored and irritated with the meeting. Suresh was not only wasting Ravi's time but also trying to show him that he was a better engineer. As soon as Praveen left the place, Suresh continued with his arguments on the correctness of the image for another five minutes. Finally, Ravi managed to convince Suresh to take Praveen's opinion before proceeding with the change.

"Ok...what are the other changes?" Ravi enquired.

"I went through your UI caching code and found that you

used an array for caching data. I changed it to use a hash-table."

"That is a major change, Suresh! Why did you do that?"

"I felt access would be faster with a hash-table. Array access is always slower, right."

"Yeah, I know that but for the amount of data that we store, it doesn't matter if we use an array or a hash-table."

"Still mine is a scalable solution."

Ravi's irritation was reaching its zenith. He still tried to sound convincing.

"Hey, that implementation has been there for two years now and we haven't faced any issues with that. There is no need for this change."

"Hmm...but still that doesn't warrant us to continue with that bad design, right."

"Bad design? Dude! What are you saying? That design worked for us for the last two years. There is nothing good or bad here. It is only about whether something is required for us or not. Also, that change you did affects the entire solution. Almost all the code!"

Listening to Ravi's statement, Suresh smiled and said, "Yeah, I know that. I made all the changes. You just have to review the code."

'What the...!' and Ravi finally tried to sound agitated. "No sane person would agree for such a change at this point of time. You can take up those changes for the next release."

But having worked under Praveen's guidance for four weeks, Suresh learnt some stuff from him. He uttered the same words that Praveen regularly used, "But next release is four months down the line, I have already made the changes. You just have to review the code. When we can get this change in for this release itself, why wait for four months?"

"But you don't understand, Suresh. That portion is tested and is a working code. We cannot make changes overnight to portions like these. Our production systems will fail if we make such abrupt changes."

"No...I have run all the tests and none of them have failed. I have added five more tests to test more scenarios and even they worked fine. I am sure that this thing will work in production."

"But our test cases do not really test all the production scenarios, right? This code has been in production for two years now and it would have been subjected to more number of scenarios than you have tested now."

"More scenarios? Can you tell me what they are?" asked Suresh.

Ravi was seething with anger now but still controlling his anger said, "I don't know but I am sure our tests do not mimic all the cases."

"Then let's go over the test list and you tell me where they are inadequate."

"Dude...I am talking with experience on my side. The moment you touch that code, you will have support calls coming right away."

"But all the tests are passing...I am fully confident that nothing will happen."

The stalemate continued for some more time. And finally when Ravi checked his watch, the time was already 7:40 p.m. That was the main reason why Ravi didn't agree for a meeting with Suresh in the morning. Any meeting with him just drags on and on like this.

'He has been arguing with me for the last one hour! Yet we haven't decided anything! God! Why don't you show me some way out.' But it looked like he himself had to do something as God seemed to be taking his own time. So finally exhausted with the discussion, Ravi said, "Dude...this way we will never reach a conclusion. Let's go to Praveen and he will tell you why we cannot do this change today."

By this time Suresh was also frustrated with Ravi as he was not agreeing with him. He agreed to take the argument to Praveen and said, "Ok...let's discuss with him then."

❖❖❖

Chapter 19

The Shock

07:45 p.m.

Just as Ravi and Suresh got up to go to Praveen's cabin, Naina's phone rang.

"Hello...Domino's Pizza delivery," said the voice from the other end of the line.

"Hello...ok! Where are you right now?"

"I am waiting at the security gate ma'am," said the person.

"Wait for 5 minutes, I will come down and collect it," said Naina and disconnected the call.

Ravi who heard the conversation volunteered to go and get the pizzas. "I will get them here. Meanwhile Suresh, you can go and start the conversation with Praveen."

Suresh agreed and said, "Ok..."

Ravi was happy that finally he could get Suresh off his back. Walking to the security gate, Ravi thought, 'Phew! That was one hell of a discussion. I have never faced someone as adamant as he is. Where does SOS recruit such people from?'

Now that he got deviated from that design discussion, Ravi started thinking about his original dinner plan. 'In the morning I thought of taking Naina to the Taj and now I am having my dinner in office. Looks like nothing in life goes as per the plan. At least I should be happy that I could keep my competitor at bay.' When the competitor is someone like your manager the joy is pleasing, so Ravi was feeling overjoyed at how he had thwarted his manager's attacks. But at the same time, a thought started disturbing him.

'Today I was successful but what about tomorrow? Will I be able to stop him?'

He started thinking about various strategies to follow for tomorrow. Thinking this way, he reached the security gate where he paid the pizza guy, and started carrying four pizzas back to his floor.

Even while walking back to his floor, his thoughts were completely focussed on what he should be doing tomorrow. But all the while nothing concrete hit him.

After getting back to his floor, he knocked on Praveen's room.

"Come in," said Praveen.

Ravi noticed that Suresh was still discussing the same issues with Praveen. "Where shall we have the dinner, Praveen? Shall we go to the cafeteria?" asked Ravi.

"No...I don't want any disturbance now. We are in the middle of our discussion," said Suresh.

"Ok...call Naina here. Let's have dinner in my cabin. Even she can participate in this meeting," said Praveen.

"I will call her then," said Ravi. He put the pizzas on Praveen's table and went out to call Naina.

"Naina...pizzas are in Praveen's room. There is a meeting going on in his room. Praveen said you can have your pizza while listening to that meeting."

"Ok..." said Naina and both of them walked to Praveen's room.

After opening the pizza boxes and deciding who gets what, the discussion on UI changes continued.

"What do you think about that hash-table change, Praveen?" asked Ravi.

"Since Suresh is confident that all the tests are passing, I think we can take that change in for this release."

Ravi's happiness on having won over his manager instantly evaporated. That kind of reaction from his boss was shocking. He protested, "We are just two days away from our deadline and you are agreeing to this change? It is a dangerous change, Praveen. We cannot accept it now..." said Ravi.

"No...no...I think it is a minor change. Just change of one data structure, right? Nothing much," said Praveen.

Even Suresh defended his change, "Yeah, right...everything works. I checked properly..."

As usual, Ravi did not agree to that argument. Meanwhile, Naina's mobile rang and seeing the number, she excused herself and went out to talk. The discussion between Ravi, Praveen and Suresh continued. Though Ravi's argument made sense to Praveen, he purposefully tried to push Ravi for reasons obvious to both of them. Ravi understood that and tried to defend his position.

Naina finished the call and entered the room. All three of them noticed that Naina was in a jubilant mood. Her face was pink with excitement.

"What Naina? You look very happy about something," asked Praveen casually.

"Yes...I am happy because my parents have finally accepted my proposal."

"What proposal?" Praveen asked.

Naina started narrating her story. "Karteek and I have been in love with each other for the last four months. Last week, he asked me if I am interested in marrying him and I agreed. Initially I feared that my parents would not agree to it and did not tell them for a week. But finally when I told them yesterday, they said they needed a day to think about it. They called me up now saying that they agree with my decision."

It was terrible news for both Ravi and Praveen. Especially for Praveen, he looked like a person who caught a live electric wire with bare hands. The pizza dropped from his hand and he sat there open-mouthed. He quickly turned to face his computer monitor and hid from others the tears that had appeared in his eyes. In a choked voice, he said, "That is good news, Naina. So, when is the marriage scheduled for?"

Naina was still in her own world and did not notice all the changes that happened around her. "The date hasn't been finalised yet. My parents will decide that after meeting with Karteek's parents."

After two similar experiences, Ravi had become immune to such situations. Also, it was just a week's love compared to the relatively long-term associations he had with his other girlfriends. Though he felt bad about how it turned out to be, he did not look like a person who was as heartbroken as Praveen. He too congratulated her by saying, "Congrats Naina. By the way who is Karteek?"

"Oh! You don't know him? He is the developer in that billing team."

Praveen knew him well. He was a developer with three years of experience and was well-known in the organisation as an efficient person. 'What? Karteek marrying Naina? What is so great about him that Naina chose him over me?' thought Praveen.

"But I thought you joined SOS only last week. How come you

know Karteek since the last four months," enquired Suresh.

"I joined SOS as a trainee four months ago. Karteek was my mentor for C# and Java. You know what? He proposed to me right on the day I joined SOS. Initially I tried to avoid him but later on I started liking him. He is such a nice guy!" said Naina.

Praveen found those praises highly discomforting. He turned towards Ravi and gave him a weak smile. Ravi did not understand the meaning of that expression, so he smiled back at Praveen. Meanwhile, Suresh finished his pizza and wiping his hands with the paper napkin said, "Congrats Naina. That was great news." Then he turned towards Ravi and Praveen, and started the discussion on his changes again.

Till that point of time, Praveen was relentlessly arguing with Ravi and trying to make him agree to the changes made by Suresh. But now after this shocking revelation from Naina, Ravi noticed a marked change in Praveen's behaviour. Praveen started defending Ravi!

"No, Suresh. We cannot do this big a change at such a late stage in our schedule. We will have to plan for such big changes properly. I agree with Ravi." Praveen's voice was still choked with all that emotional turmoil he had just gone through.

It was now Suresh's turn to go pale. He had spent three sleepless nights to get this thing working. "But Praveen it took me three nights to get this working. I haven't even slept properly over the last few days," he said.

Praveen was already in a bad mood and the statement from Suresh irked him more. "If you have had so much time to rewrite so many codes, you should have told me. I would have assigned you more meaningful work. You have wasted three days, Suresh!"

That one statement from his manager was enough to push

Suresh into a tricky situation. Arguing with a manager who sounded so irritated did not make any sense to him and he said, "Ok...but I thought it would improve the quality of our code."

"Keep those changes aside, we can use them later. Save them somewhere and register a bug on this issue. We can push them in our next release."

"Ok..." said Suresh who had now gone calm.

Ravi now felt that he had at least something to feel good about. After two years of working with Praveen, it was the first time he was speaking on Ravi's side. 'Not once did he ever agree with me. Today's shock seems to have changed him. Though I have lost Naina, my work life will improve a bit now,' he thought.

Also, being a Shahrukh fan, Ravi believed in wooing a girl even after she is engaged to someone else. Shahrukh Khan made him realise that hope is the most important of all the factors that are required when it comes to dealing with love. That was the reason why he had watched DDLJ around thirty times and today he was planning to watch some other movies of Shahrukh Khan to get some new ideas on how he could still woo Naina to his side. Though he tried this on his first girlfriend, his plans hadn't worked because of his inexperience. But now with some experience on his side, he thought, 'I can be successful this time.' That confidence was what kept him going. But poor Praveen wasn't thinking on those lines. He looked like 'Devdas' in the guise of a software engineer.

Naina finished her pizza and left the room. Suresh and Ravi left the room as soon as Praveen did not agree to Suresh's changes. And depressed with such an unexpected turn of events, Praveen did not finish his pizza and threw it into the dustbin.

❖❖❖

Chapter 20

The Manager's Tale

09:00 p.m.

Though Ravi was disturbed, he was happy that Suresh was shown his place by Praveen. He got another forty minutes of uninterrupted time to complete his work. Ravi was also consoled by the fact that this time he was not alone in his grief. Just at this moment his outlook calendar reminded him of the meeting with Carl at 9:00 p.m. He got up from his seat and walked to the conference room 4138 which is where all the meetings with Carl were normally scheduled.

Ravi opened the door of the conference room and walked in. Only Praveen was present in the room and he still had that sad expression on his face. 'Dude, hasn't come out of the shock yet,' thought Ravi. Not knowing what to do, Ravi tried to start a conversation with Praveen.

"So Praveen, what is the agenda. Is it just about Silverlight, or about anything else also?"

"I think it will be only about Silverlight. I have already told him in the mail about what extra items we are planning to take up and what we are leaving behind."

Ravi took one final aim at shooting down Silverlight for this release. "Praveen, do you really think we can take up Silverlight for this release? It is very difficult, I don't think I can handle it in a week."

To his surprise Praveen replied, "Yeah...for the past one hour that is what I have been thinking too. It might be difficult to handle Silverlight in this release. Let's properly plan and do it over the next one month. Ravi, you can take the whole of the next week to read the book that I gave you. We can schedule that presentation of yours next to the next Monday."

Ravi felt like hugging Praveen. 'Wow! One bad experience has transformed him into an angel. But why has he become so friendly all of a sudden?' thought Ravi.

Suresh entered the room with a coffee cup in his hand and sat in a chair quietly. He was still ruminating over the way Praveen dealt with him today. Naina was the last one to enter the room and she too sat quietly.

"So, shall we begin," said Praveen and everyone nodded in acceptance.

Praveen put the phone in the speaker mode and dialled Carl's number.

"Hello..."

"Hi Carl...this is Praveen and team from SOS," said Praveen.

"Hi guys! So, what is that you want to discuss with me?"

Ravi picked up the conversation. "It is about the Silverlight requirement, Carl. Do we need to do it for this release?"

"No...if you think we cannot do it by this Friday, let's take it in our next release. It is not mandatory," said Carl.

Praveen chipped in and said, "Yeah, right...even I was thinking that we should take it up for our next release."

"I agree," said Ravi.

"Ok then...let's move onto the other work items. How are the UI tests coming along?" asked Carl.

Before Ravi could answer anything Praveen got in and said,

"All the priority '1' cases have been addressed, Carl. I think Ravi and Naina will complete all the other cases by Friday. We are on track."

"That is great! Praveen, you have signed up for some more new items, right?"

"Yes."

"Are you sure you can deliver them by Friday?"

"Yes...I am sure," said Praveen.

"Great! Is there anything else?"

"Nothing more," said Praveen.

"Ok then...bye guys. Good night," said Carl and disconnected the call.

Though Suresh made up his mind in the morning to discuss his changes with Carl, he changed his decision based on the kind of feedback he got from Praveen. 'If Praveen scolded me so much, Carl will definitely blast me. It would be better if I keep away from it,' thought Suresh and kept quiet throughout the meeting. As soon as the call was over, he got up and walked away.

Naina too got up picking up her cellphone and walked to her desk. By the time Praveen and Ravi walked out of the room, they noticed that she was busy conversing with someone on the phone.

'She is definitely conversing with Karteek,' thought Praveen and turned towards Ravi. "Can you come to my room once," he said and walked away.

Ravi walked to his cubicle collected his stuff and then walked to Praveen's cabin. As usual, he knocked on the door and Praveen said, "Come in..."

As he walked in, he noticed that Praveen had packed his belongings and was ready to leave for the day. 'What does he want to discuss with me now?' thought Ravi and stood there waiting.

"Ravi...both of us know what went on between us since the morning...right?" said Praveen.

Ravi was surprised to see his manager being so open about what had happened. He agreed with some hesitation, "Yeah, correct..."

Praveen's voice choked up again. Controlling tears with utmost difficulty he said, "I thought I would be successful, Ravi. I am not feeling comfortable now. I was planning to go to the pub for a drink. Care to join me?"

Ravi now understood why his manager was trying to be so friendly with him for the last one hour or so. 'He wanted someone to accompany him to the pub. Dude seems to be too shaken with the whole episode...but it looks like he is 'Devdas' and I am his pet dog. What shall I do?' he thought.

Ravi was thinking about an answer for it when Praveen asked him again, "Are you coming?"

Thinking about home, Ravi suddenly remembered Ganesh's words. 'I will drink 'Redbull' and wait for you. Today you will feel the power of my punches.' Those words gave him one reason to go the pub.

'The only way I can counter Ganesh's 'Redbull' is with beer,' he thought. Ganesh was a teetotaller who was scared of guys who were drunk. Ravi never knew the exact reason for that, but Ganesh always maintained distance from such people. 'I will drink so much that I will drop asleep as soon as I reach the apartment's doorstep. How will he kick me then?' he thought and finally agreed.

"Ok...I will come with you. But who will drop me home?"

"I will drop you. No issues..." Praveen assured him.

And both of them got down to the car park and got into Praveen's car.

"Praveen...one request...I need to collect my pen drive from Gate 1."

"No problem, I will drive from that gate," said Praveen. Ravi collected his pen drive and Praveen started driving to the nearest pub in the Madhapur area which was very near to Gachibowli.

"Terrible news, isn't it?" asked Praveen.

"Yeah...I did not expect such a turn of events."

"This is the first time something like this ever happened to me, you know. How about you?"

"Second time," Ravi did not want to talk about that on-site love story now.

"Ok...so you must be feeling worse then?" enquired Praveen.

"On the contrary, I somehow got used to this stuff. Not as painful as it was the first time."

"Oh, is it? I think it will take me at least a month to get out of this shock..." said Praveen, and Ravi thought he saw tears in Praveen's eyes.

'Why is he getting so emotional? It is just the first time that he failed and that too it has been only one week that Naina joined our team. God! Can't he take even one failure?' thought Ravi.

"No problem, Praveen. Be cheerful. You will get a better girlfriend," Ravi tried to cheer him up. Praveen stopped talking and appeared to be in deep thought.

It was 10:00 p.m. by the time they reached the pub. Praveen dropped Ravi at the gate and went around finding a parking slot.

For the moment, Praveen's grief made Ravi become a stronger person. 'I am consoling my boss who is seven years older than me. I have to sound mature,' he thought. But he failed to notice that his boss was acting childish.

After Praveen parked the car, they entered the pub and chose a table. Having already decided that he will drink to his limits, Ravi ordered a pitcher of beer. Praveen was in no mood for beer. He started ordering a variety of cocktails and some other harder stuff. Noticing that his boss was planning to drink more than he had planned for, Ravi changed his goal for the day.

'At least one of us has to stay awake to take the other person home. If he drinks this way I should carry him. It is better if I stop with a glass of beer,' thought Ravi.

Ravi slowly started sipping his stuff whereas his manager was treating everything on that table as a shot. Be it a glass or a bottle or a shot, everything was getting finished in a matter of seconds. After getting drunk to a level where the alcohol started showing noticeable effect on his mind, Praveen slowed down.

"I have never felt so sad in my life before," said Praveen in a thick voice which indicated that he was heavily drunk.

"But Praveen, it is just a week's love. Why are you feeling so bad about it?" questioned Ravi.

"It is not about whether it is a week's love or a month's love, Ravi. It is the magnitude of heartburn that the incident causes which matters. It is the first time I did anything like this, man! Not even in college did I try something like this. I have always concentrated on my career till now. I never even had the time to think about love or marriage or girls."

"Ok!" said Ravi and unable to think of anything that could console Praveen, he kept quiet.

"You know what? Three months ago I crossed thirty-two years. These days not even a single girl is replying to my profile on *'shaadi.com'*," the anger clearly showed in Praveen's voice. "These days everyone prefers a younger groom. This way I will have to settle for an aunty someday."

"No, Praveen...I don't think the marriage market is that bad. I think you are a highly eligible bachelor. If Bollywood heroes who are into their late forties can be eligible bachelors, you are eligible too. You are earning well, have a car, you are a manager and you are good-looking too." Having said that Ravi thought, 'Good-looking! Maybe, I shouldn't have said that. I think he is just about average looking.'

Though Ravi's words were to Praveen's liking, still they did not have the power to pull him off from his depression. "What is the use of all that, Ravi? Five months ago, some bride's family contacted our family and asked us about my details. When we told them that I earn around 10 lakh rupees per annum, they said it is too less for a manager of my age and said goodbye. Working in this high stress environment, I am losing my hair too. Who will give me a bride if it continues like this?" questioned Praveen.

Ravi now understood why Praveen was so heartbroken, 'He is thinking that he will never get a good bride.' Ravi said, "Oh! That is bad..." Also Praveen's revelations were a big shock to Ravi. 'Man! This marriage market seems to be too competitive. Why is it that in India we boys have to compete for everything? Marks, engineering seats, jobs and now even brides and girlfriends!'

Having downed another glass of drink, Praveen continued, "Yeah...these days, girls' parents have become too intelligent. And girls have become too choosy. Girls want handsome grooms who are in their twenties and the girl's parents want someone who is earning a good amount. Wherefrom I will get such a salary in this recession time?"

"Yeah, you are correct..."

"And on top of that, it seems, some idiot from my group had complained to Ramnath about my behaviour. A promotion which was due since a long time was not given to me because of that reason," said Praveen.

Ravi was surprised as well as shocked. He thought Ramnath hadn't taken any action on his report but it seemed to have worked. 'Finally, Praveen got his due...' he thought and controlling his smile said, "Oh! Is it? Do you know who registered that complaint?"

Praveen was now talking with half-closed eyes. "Hic! No... Ramnath did not tell me but I think it is Naresh...he quarrels with me regularly... If not for that complaint...I would have taken less work for this release. Now that my promotion got dinged, I had to continue working hard and show them that I can still execute well."

Ravi's smile evaporated into thin air. He realised that his complaint had boomeranged on him. 'What! I screwed up my own life? What a life! Whether I complain or not, it is ultimately I, who is becoming the ass,' he thought.

Meanwhile, Praveen continued, "Next...review...cycle...I will show Naresh...what...I can do... By the way...are you not going to finish the content...in that pitcher?"

"No...I have had enough," said Ravi.

"Then...I will finish it," said Praveen and started pouring the contents into his glass.

Seeing Praveen's state, Ravi got a bit nervous. "Hey Praveen! I think it is enough. You are drinking too much. I think you should stop," said Ravi.

"Hic! One last glass..." said Praveen and continued his rants.

"Hic! You see the way Naina fell for that idiot Karteek... That fellow is good for nothing...except that he goes to gym daily and maintains a body... Hic! People like us work hard...and see what we get... NOTHING!" shouted Praveen.

Some people in the pub who were still in their senses turned to see what had happened. Ravi was getting embarrassed with the behaviour of Praveen and he tried to control him. "Things like these are common, Praveen. You are unnecessarily taking them to the heart. Leave it..."

"NO RAVI... Hic! I WILL HAVE THAT FELLOW FIRED... THINKS HE CAN STEAL MY GIRL," Praveen started shouting. Ravi did not know how to control Praveen who seemed to be getting agitated with every passing moment.

"Hic! Just because...he is young, she chooses him... is it? WHAT SHOULD HAPPEN TO GUYS LIKE US?" and Praveen gulped another glass of beer.

The pub management also seemed to be noticing it and Ravi felt that they would send someone soon enough to kick them out of the bar. So he tried his best to control Praveen and said, "Karteek was fast, Praveen. He proposed to her right on the first day. We were late. Maybe, next time you should propose to someone while conducting the interview itself." And he smiled thinking that Praveen would appreciate his joke.

Praveen downed another glass and surely was in no mood to appreciate anything. He took an empty bottle present on the table and broke it against the table. He stood up, held the broken piece high and shouted again, "Hic! I WILL KILL THAT *******..."

Ravi was frightened to see such a reaction from his manager. Meanwhile, when Praveen broke the bottle so violently, some of the splinters fell on someone sitting nearby. The person onto whom the splinters fell got angry. He got up and rushed to their table. He caught hold of Praveen by his collar and slapped him once. Praveen fell down on the floor and while making an attempt to stand up started crawling on the floor. Unable to support himself on all the four limbs, he decided to give up his struggle to stand up and finally fell flat on the floor. Seeing that his manager was being beaten up by some random guy, Ravi rushed to Praveen's rescue.

"Hey stop! He is drunk. He did not do that intentionally," Ravi shouted. The other fellow was so pissed off with the happenings that he was in no mood to listen to anyone and now turned his ire onto Ravi. Before Ravi could utter another word both his cheeks had turned red. The man had managed to implant his fingerprints on Ravi's cheeks too. Tears welled up in Ravi's eyes instantly.

Seeing the commotion, the bartenders were religiously dispatched to their table and they took control of the situation. They pulled away the man from the location, and caught hold of Praveen and made him stand up. They ordered both the parties to leave the premises immediately.

Ravi was on the verge of crying. He noticed that people were watching them and it made the situation worse. He noticed some good-looking girls in the pub smiling and felt that they were cracking some jokes at his expense. He did not want to stay there anymore. Controlling his tears, he requested the tenders to bring the bill so that he could settle it. Along with the bill, he asked them to bring a bottle of beer which he wanted to consume at home.

The bartenders made Praveen sit in his place and pulled that broken bottle of his hand. The other person who had just managed to beat them was in an inebriated state himself and continued his quarrel with the bar management.

But Praveen who had managed to start all this was in a different world. He was unmindful of the fact that someone had slapped him and that he was being thrown out of a bar. He had reached his limit and he slowly fell asleep. But still in that sleepy state, he was murmuring, "I will kill that *******..."

❖❖❖

Chapter 21

The Day Never Ends

11:15 p.m.

Ravi was stuck with his unconscious manager in a pub. He was still unable to come to terms with what had happened. 'Never was I slapped by anyone. Even my dad had never slapped me and today I got slapped by some idiot and that too for no mistake of mine. All because of the overreaction from Praveen...#$@!#@#. He made me a laughing stock.' Ravi started scolding his boss. But what is the use of scolding a person who is as drunk as Praveen was. At that moment, there was no difference between him and a log.

After five minutes, the bill was delivered to him. Looking at the amount mentioned in the bill, Ravi's eyes almost popped out. 'Eight thousand three hundred rupees including taxes' read the bill. Ravi did not even understand the names of half the stuff listed on that paper. 'My God! What stuff did Praveen drink today?' thought Ravi and having no other option pulled out his credit card and paid the bill. But he preserved the receipt with the intention of getting the amount reimbursed from Praveen tomorrow.

Now he faced the biggest of all the challenges. 'How do I take him home? I don't know how to drive a four-wheeler,' thought Ravi. Added to it, Ravi did not know Praveen's residential address. So Ravi pulled out his cellphone and called Naresh, who he thought might know Praveen's address.

"Hello..."

"Yeah, hi...why did you call me at such an odd hour?" asked Naresh.

"Nothing. Praveen drank a bit too much today and has fallen asleep. Need to drop him at his home. Do you know his address?" asked Ravi.

"What? Both of you went to a pub?" asked Naresh in a surprised tone.

"I will explain everything to you tomorrow. Now tell me whether you know his address or at least his residential telephone number?"

"I don't know. Try calling Suresh, maybe he knows his number," advised Naresh.

Ravi was in no mood to call Suresh and that too at such an odd hour in the night. "Dude...if I call him he will drag the discussion for another one hour. Anyway...I will find some other way."

"Ok...good luck..." said Naresh and disconnected the call.

'What should I do now?' thought Ravi. After thinking for a minute, he hit upon an idea. He pulled out Praveen's cellphone from his pocket and browsed through the contacts' list to search for some name like 'dad' or 'home'. Ravi was lucky that night as he found a contact named 'home' in the list.

He dialled that number and someone picked up the phone and said, "Hello."

"Hello," replied Ravi, "hi...Is this Praveen's home?"

"Yes..." replied the voice.

"I am Praveen's colleague. There has been a party at our place today and Praveen got a bit drunk. Could you please tell me your address so that I can drop him?"

"What is your name?" asked the voice from the other end.

"My name is Ravi. May I know who am I talking to?"

"I am Praveen's dad," said the voice.

"Sir...can you tell me the address please. We are in Madhapur right now."

"Ok...note it down," said Praveen's dad and gave him the address of some apartment in the Banjara Hills area. As Ravi was about to disconnect the call, he thought he heard him shout to Praveen's mother, "Your son has fallen drunk somewhere. What a shame!"

Ravi had never seen Praveen as a peer but today's experience made him see his manager in new light. 'He has the same life as I have,' he thought and switched his thoughts towards transport options.

'What are the options before me?' thought Ravi and the only option that he could think of was an auto.

Coming out of the pub, Ravi noticed that the road was empty. The bartenders were courteous enough to carry Praveen to the gate and leave him there. Praveen was sitting on the pavement and still murmuring, "I will kill...I will fire..."

After waiting for ten minutes like that, Ravi noticed an empty auto coming their way and he stopped it.

"Banjara Hills Road number 11 and then to Ameerpet," said Ravi.

"For whom?" asked the *auto-wallah*.

Ravi said, “I and the person sitting there...” and showed Praveen sitting on the pavement.

“That will be 500 rupees.”

“What? 500 rupees!!!”

“Yes...500.”

“I will pay you double the meter. Nothing more...” Ravi sounded adamant.

“Sir...it is 11:30 now. You will not get another auto if you leave me. Double the meter is for normal trips. You people are drunk and any other *auto-wallah* would also ask you for the same amount if not more.”

“Ok...I will pay you 300,” Ravi tried to bargain.

“No sir...450,” and the bargaining spree continued. Finally Ravi and the *auto-wallah* struck a deal for 375 rupees.

Having pushed Praveen into the auto, Ravi directed the auto to Praveen’s apartments first.

The night was a pleasant one and the cool breeze managed to revive Praveen a bit. He noticed that Ravi was helping him get back home. Tears welled up in his eyes and in a choked voice he started talking. His voice was thick indicating that he was heavily drunk. He said, “You are a...true friend... You...are helping... me...”

With experience Ravi knew that most people who talk to him like that in their drunken stupor actually forget about all that once they get up in the morning. So, Ravi did not get carried away with that reaction from his manager. He said, “No issues, Praveen. My house is also somewhere nearby, so dropping you is not a big issue.”

Praveen was neither listening to him nor trying to listen to anyone. He just continued, "You...are helping me...I love you, my friend...I love you." And in that inebriated state, he pulled Ravi's face towards himself and kissed him on his cheeks and continued muttering, "I love you...I love you..."

Ravi was shocked with the sudden development. He tried to wriggle out of Praveen's grasp but Praveen was not letting him go. Ravi noticed that the auto driver was turning back repeatedly and watching the happenings with a shocked look on his face. With each passing moment, Ravi was getting more and more embarrassed.

"Drive faster," he shouted to the auto driver. To his luck Praveen's apartments showed up in ten minutes. There he handed over Praveen to the watchman at the gate and heaved a sigh of relief. He started his journey back home and he felt a bit more relaxed now.

'What a turn of events. I thought I would go on a date with a girl and finally it turned out to be something like 'Dostana'. Hope that none other than this auto driver saw what had happened today. In the morning I thought paying 150 rupees for my commute to office was high and took a shared auto. And now because of Praveen I am poorer by 400 bucks. Bullshit!' thought Ravi.

Till now he hadn't thought much about what Ganesh would do to him, but now that he was getting nearer to his apartments, fear started to mount. He had been careful enough to buy a bottle of beer at the pub and it was still with him.

'If Ganesh shows me that 'Redbull' of his, I will drink this bottle right in front of him. Then we shall see who gets scared of whom.' The auto neared his apartment and Ravi could see that almost everyone in his apartments was fast asleep. Only a light here and a light there were on, and the one prominent among all of them was the light glowing in the balcony of his apartment.

He could see someone sitting in the balcony and watching the auto which was coming to a halt near the apartments. From the silhouette in the balcony, he could make out that it was Ganesh. 'Obviously, he is waiting for me,' he thought.

Ravi got down from the auto and paid the *auto-wallah* who started demanding for more now.

"I thought these apartments were somewhere near the main road. They are so much in the interior. Now I will leave only if you pay me 450 rupees," he demanded.

Ravi was shocked with the sudden demand from the *auto-wallah*. 'What the...? We agreed on a price and now he is demanding more...'

Ravi counted 375 rupees and put that money in the driver's hand and said, "This is it. I am not paying you more."

The driver did not listen and started shouting and cursing Ravi. "I won't take it. I will leave only if you pay me 450 rupees," said the driver and stuck to that place.

"I told you where exactly both the locations were. Why are you demanding more now?" Ravi questioned.

The *auto-wallah* had an instant reply. "I thought both of you were normal people. Seeing all that stuff you did in my auto I am demanding more."

Ravi noticed that the guards were standing nearby. He thought that the events were getting more and more complicated and it was useless to argue with the driver and make him shout more stuff. So he said, "Ok...I don't have more change. Will get it after going to my apartment." He left thinking, 'This is a huge apartment complex. Where will this guy search for me once I get into my flat?' And laughing to himself he had one good glance at the balcony from where Ganesh was watching all the drama.

Thinking about how he should deal with Ganesh and finish his day with a nice Shahrukh Khan movie, Ravi pressed the button for the lifts.

❖❖❖